She couldn't stop touching him

She seemed to crave the contact. It was only because they were trapped here together, Cassie told herself. Because he was the only other person in this remote place, and they needed each other to survive. Yet she knew that didn't fully explain the tightness in her throat. The worry. The fear of losing him. She felt all things for Thorn, whether she admitted it or not.

Awake, he'd been forceful. Sleeping now, he looked peaceful. And defenseless. Cassie couldn't stop herself from gently touching his lips. They moved against her fingers, responding to the contact, and the movement sent a shiver up her arm.

Who was this man who seemed so lost one moment and so sure of himself the next? Why was he hiding here?

"You're in trouble, aren't you?" she whispered. And then she knew. "We're both in trouble."

REBECCA YORK

USA TODAY bestselling author Ruth Glick published her one hundredth book, *Crimson Moon,* a Berkley Sensation, in January 2005. Her latest 43 Light Street book is *The Secret Night,* published in April 2006. In October she launches the Harlequin Intrigue continuity series SECURITY BREACH with *Chain Reaction.*

Ruth's many honors include two RITA® Award finalist books. She has two Career Achievement Awards from *Romantic Times BOOKclub* for Series Romantic Suspense and Series Romantic Mystery. *Nowhere Man* was the *Romantic Times BOOKclub* Best Intrigue of 1998 and is one of their "all-time favorite 400 romances." Ruth's *Killing Moon* and *Witching Moon* both won the New Jersey Romance Writers Golden Leaf Award for Paranormal.

Michael Dirda of *Washington Post Book World* says, "Her books...deliver what they promise—excitement, mystery, romance."

Since 1997 she has been writing on her own as Rebecca York. Between 1990 and 1997 she wrote the Light Street series with Eileen Buckholtz. You can contact Ruth at rglick@capaccess.org or visit her Web site at www.rebeccayork.com.

43 LIGHT STREET

REBECCA YORK

Prince of Time

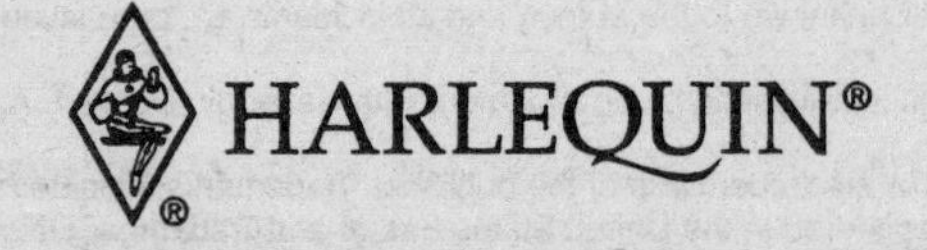

TORONTO • NEW YORK • LONDON
AMSTERDAM • PARIS • SYDNEY • HAMBURG
STOCKHOLM • ATHENS • TOKYO • MILAN • MADRID
PRAGUE • WARSAW • BUDAPEST • AUCKLAND

ISBN-13: 978-0-373-36065-9
ISBN-10: 0-373-36065-7

PRINCE OF TIME

This edition published by arrangement with Harlequin Books S.A.

www.eHarlequin.com

Printed in U.S.A.

Directory

43 LIGHT STREET

	Room
ADVENTURES IN TRAVEL	204
ABIGAIL FRANKLIN, Ph.D. Clinical Psychology	509
BIRTH DATA, Inc.	322
INNER HARBOR PRODUCTIONS	404
THE LIGHT STREET FOUNDATION	322
KATHRYN MARTIN-McQUADE, M.D. Branch Office, Medizone Labs	515
O'MALLEY & LANCER Detective Agency	518
LAURA ROSWELL, LL.B. Attorney at Law	311
SABRINA'S FANCY	Lobby
STRUCTURAL DESIGN GROUP	407
NOEL ZACHARIAS Paralegal Service	311
L. ROSSINI Superintendent	Lower Level

CAST OF CHARACTERS

Cassandra Devereaux—On an expedition to Alaska, she met the man of her dreams.

Thorn—He was a stranger in a strange land. And his time was running out.

Jacques Montague—Collecting artifacts was his passion. Amassing power, his obsession.

Marie Pindel—Where did her loyalty lie?

Lodar—He took revenge on anyone who got in his way.

Zeke Chambers—Had he stumbled on the find of the century or a very clever fake?

Feydor Lenov—The Russian followed orders—for a price.

Victor Kirkland—The State Department official was playing two operations close to his vest.

Marissa Devereaux—She'd do anything to save her sister.

Chapter One

One moment she was exhilarated, excited, trembling on the brink of discovery. In the next, an ominous rumble on the mountain far above her told Cassandra Devereaux she was going to die.

Glen Fielding, her Alaskan guide, was already running.

Early this morning he'd landed his float plane on a clear blue lake a hundred miles northwest of Denali National Park. And Cassie had been awed by the rugged peaks and endless green of the Douglas firs as she and Glen paddled his canoe to shore and hiked a couple of miles through the wilderness to this remote slope.

Glen was twenty feet below her and on the right, but it was already too late for either of them to escape.

Cassandra screamed as several tons of last winter's snow came rumbling down the mountain like a glacier broken loose from its moorings. This wasn't supposed to happen. Not in summer.

She gasped Glen's name as he disappeared under a blanket of white. Lumps of ice pelted her head and shoulders before she ducked under the shelter of a protective ledge. The mountain shook like a fortress under aerial bombardment, and she waited for the tumbling snow and boulders to sweep her away.

As suddenly as the avalanche had started, it stopped, leaving Cassie crouched in eerie silence. Cautiously, she moved her arms and legs. The worst pain she detected was in her right arm, but it was bearable.

"Glen? Glen?"

He didn't answer.

She tried to struggle forward, tried to get to the spot where he'd disappeared. But she was trapped by a solid wall of white.

A choking sensation clogged Cassie's throat. Ignoring it, she found her pack under a rock and scrabbled through the contents, cursing when she remembered that Glen had taken the trench shovel. Grimly, she set a flashlight on a pile of snow and started digging. But after a few minutes, her fingers stiff from the cold, she could see that her efforts only brought more snow down on her head.

Breathing hard, she snatched up the light and searched the pack again, looking for the two-way radio. The case was broken. When she twisted the dials, there wasn't even a crackle of static.

Cassie hugged her shoulders and leaned back against the rock wall of her prison. At least she was alive, she told herself. For now.

But what about Glen, she wondered with a stab of guilt. She had a pilot's license. She could have flown here herself. But she'd wanted to look like nothing more than a travel agent, so she'd paid well for Glen's services. She hadn't told him she was on a highly classified assignment from the government. Instead she'd used the cover story she and her sister, Marissa, found so convenient—that they specialized in scouting out adventure locales. And she'd been hired by a millionaire sportsman in the lower forty-eight who wanted to climb a mountain nobody else had tackled.

As she and Glen had approached the Alaskan range, her special instruments had confirmed that there was something strange on the east slope of one of the peaks.

"Never taken anyone here before," her guide had remarked as he set the plane down on the water with a gentle touch.

"That's what my client wants," Cassie had replied cheerfully, trying to mask the excitement in her voice. This expedition was important to her, more important than she was willing to admit.

Now look what she'd gotten herself into, she thought as she fought panic. Nobody knew where she was. No one was going to come rescue her the way Jed Prentiss had saved her sister a few months ago. With a fleeting smile, she thought about Jed and Marci, taking comfort from the knowledge that her sister was well and happy. At least one of the Devereaux sisters had escaped the ravages of their childhood.

But that childhood had also made them both fighters. And Cassie wasn't going to give up so easily. Pulling out her flashlight, she started inching along the ledge, squeezing around a boulder that had crashed against the rock. Behind it was a large indentation and, on the ground, shards of what might have been basalt. Only they looked too jagged.

Cassie picked one up, running her thumb cautiously along the edge. It felt more like plastic than stone. Turning, she realized that light emanated from the hole the boulder had made. When she shouldered the cracked surface, it gave with a groaning sound, and she stumbled through—into some sort of manmade corridor. The walls were cold metal, but they radiated a gentle amber glow like an old computer screen.

Dear heaven! It looked as if the boulder had crashed into an escape hatch for a secret military post. The irony made her laugh, the sound echoing hollowly off the tunnel walls. So much for the FCC's little mystery! They were going to be angry about spending the money to send her up here.

Cassandra expected to hear alarms ring and see guards with machine guns. But there was no intruder alert, only the insistent hum of equipment deep in the earth.

"Anybody home?"

Only the hollow echo of her own voice answered. Maybe this was an automated facility. Replacing her flashlight in her pack, she crept forward, aware that the humming was getting louder as she descended into the mountain. Several feet ahead of her, the passage was dark. But as she moved forward, the glow kept pace, imparting an eerie sense of being ushered onward.

Yet she couldn't detect the video cameras that must be marking her progress. And she found herself fighting a growing sense that she'd stepped into a science-fiction movie. The very air smelled as if it had been scrubbed by special purification equipment and recycled for centuries.

Shivering, she tried to put aside such fantasies. This place couldn't have been here for centuries. It had almost certainly been built as part of our Soviet surveillance network.

Her progress stopped abruptly at a flat metal door with no handle. Now what? She didn't have a key card. And there was no way her retinal patterns or handprints were in the computer. Trying the old-fashioned method, she banged on the door. When nothing happened, she began to look for a control panel. Maybe she'd find a phone, and she could call for help. There had to be something! She couldn't have come so far only to be shut out.

Doggedly, she went over every inch of the metal walls, pressing and feeling for invisible seams. She wasn't sure which random motion had the desired effect, but a sudden whooshing noise made her look up to see twin panels glide out of the way like the doors on the starship *Enterprise.*

Beyond was a yawning, profound blackness, alive with the pulsing sound she'd been hearing since she'd entered the tunnel. The unknown waited for her inside, and she was afraid. But in the end, there was really no choice. Gathering her courage, she crossed the threshold.

As before, the lights came up, and she saw that she was in what looked like a control room, surrounded by banks of futuristic computers and other equipment she couldn't identify. In the center of the room was a tall chamber about the size of a telephone booth.

Curiosity—or perhaps a feeling of compulsion—drew Cassie toward the enclosed space. Its walls were opaque and shot through with streaks of color like mother-of-pearl. Afraid, yet fascinated, Cassie watched as they began to glow and change, becoming translucent—the transformation coming from the top down.

The humming of the equipment increased, rising to

a crescendo around her, but she hardly heard. All her attention was focused on the compartment before her. *Someone was inside.* She saw the eyes first. Was transfixed by the laser intensity that held her captive, compelling her to take a step forward and then another to meet her destiny.

Blood pounding in her ears, she stood immobile as the walls of the chamber went through a final metamorphosis. Before her motionless gaze, they turned transparent as glass. And she found herself staring in shock at a naked man.

He didn't respond to her sharp intake of breath, and she realized with stunned certainty and a degree of relief that those probing eyes were not looking at her. In fact, although she stood only six feet away, he didn't seem aware that anyone else was in the room. Was it possible that only *she* could see *him* through the transparent surface separating them? The supposition gave her a measure of reassurance as anger flashed across his rigid features, anger that rolled from him in an almost physical wave, penetrating the chamber, crashing against the walls and ceiling of the small room.

Cassie wanted to turn and run. Get away from him before he shattered the walls of the capsule, charged out and blocked her escape. But some almost supernatural force kept her from turning away from the threat he represented. In that moment she was sure that he had compelled her to this place. But her mind couldn't cope with such an outlandish assumption, and she dismissed it.

She worried her lip and wiped her damp palms on the legs of her jogging pants as she stood and watched him. His face was strong, the features pleasing and vaguely exotic. Cassie studied the slight slant of his eyes, the exaggerated thrust of his chin, the wide mouth, wondering if he came from some tribe of Native Americans that barely interacted with the outside world. Was that it? Did his people live up here in the Alaskan wilds? Had they built this place? If so, why was he imprisoned?

His posture was erect and still as a statue, and she had an even wilder thought—that he was a prince from another time and place thrown into a trance by an evil sorcerer. He'd been under this mountain for centuries, waiting. And she was the woman sent to wake him with a kiss.

The fantasy was getting personal again. She shook her head to banish it. But still, she couldn't tug her gaze from him. She watched as he drew in a shuddering breath, filling his lungs greedily and then exhaling with more control. Slowly, he raised his hand and flexed the fingers, looking at them with a slightly bemused expression. Raising the hand farther, he flattened the palm against his chest, pressing it over his heart as if needing reassurance that life was surging through his veins. He let out a deep sigh. Then his face changed, the features taking on a sudden wrenching vulnerability that made her own heart contract.

Transfixed, she watched as his palm slid across his chest, across skin that was a light copper and covered with a mat of curly hair that was almost black. Before she had time to reflect on the strangeness of the combination, the hand moved, sweeping lower down. Her gaze was compelled to follow as he briefly touched his flat stomach, narrow waist, strong thighs and finally the male part of him. With a swallow, Cassie silently acknowledged that he would have drawn appreciative stares on a nude beach.

The observation jerked her befuddled brain back to reality. He wasn't on some California beach. This guy was standing buck-naked in the middle of a secret government facility. Or was it an asylum for the criminally insane with him as the star inmate? She didn't know what she'd walked into—but she was getting the heck out.

She took a step back. Before she could turn to run, his eyes caught the movement, and she knew without doubt that the capsule was as transparent from inside as well as out. At first he'd been absorbed with himself, like a sleeper awakening in a strange place. Now his gaze locked with hers, and she realized he was suddenly aware that he wasn't alone in the room.

His lips moved urgently. He appeared to be shouting at her, but she could hear nothing. At the quick shake of her head, his mouth formed a harsh line. Then he closed his eyes as his fingers felt rapidly along the sides of his prison, doubtless searching for a release latch. Thankfully, Cassie couldn't see one. She wanted him safe on the other side of that transparent barrier. Her relief was short-lived. He touched some hidden mechanism she hadn't spotted, and the front panel of his isolation booth slid silently open.

She gasped as the invisible wall disappeared. She gasped again as he stepped out of the compartment. There was no hesitation. She was his quarry. Freed, he closed the distance between them with such speed that his movements were almost a blur. His hand shot out and circled her wrist, his fingers rigid as a steel manacle.

"Don't hurt me." Her mouth was so dry she could

hardly force the words out. Why hadn't she gotten out of this place when the getting was good?

Up close, his eyes were a startling blue. As he studied her, they turned the color of frost, making her fear shoot up several degrees. He answered her plea with a short burst of syllables that would have been melodious if his voice hadn't sounded like broken glass. She didn't know the language—and she'd studied half a dozen in college and graduate school. Yet she recognized from the inflection that he was asking a question. And that he was angry—as if she were somehow to blame for imprisoning him in that strange tube.

She shook her head, all the while struggling to wrench from his grasp. But it was as futile as trying to fight a force of nature.

She moved as far away as the extension of her arm would allow, her eyes never leaving his. She was grateful that he didn't pull her closer.

Speaking slowly and distinctly as though addressing a child, he repeated the string of syllables. The speed of the delivery, however, did nothing for her level of comprehension. There was absolutely nothing she recognized.

"I—I'm sorry. I don't understand."

His eyes narrowed, and she felt the physical force of his pent-up anger and frustration. He spoke again, and she could tell that he was demanding an answer, perhaps even threatening her if she didn't cooperate. Yet at the same time she sensed he'd given up hope of commanding her cooperation.

"I'm sorry. Please—"

"Klat!" The ugly syllable erupted from him. She didn't know what it meant, but she recognized a curse when she heard it.

Cassie sucked in a deep breath and let it out slowly. Now it was her turn. "Who are you?" she asked, repeating the question as slowly as he had spoken—in Spanish, German, French, Russian and slightly shaky Japanese. Too bad she didn't know Klingon.

Not even a flicker of recognition crossed his strong features. His answer was as unintelligible as his prior attempt at communication. Still clasping her wrist, he stepped closer, taking in details the way she had done so recently. Only now he wasn't separated from her by a barrier.

He was dynamic—and very naked—and standing so near that she could smell the masculine scent of his body and take in the fine lines radiating from the corners of his eyes. His scrutiny almost shattered her carefully forged composure.

She swallowed. At least his closeness meant she didn't have to keep her gaze from wandering to certain parts of his anatomy. All she could see was his naked arms. His naked chest. But she remembered the rest. Very well.

She stood as still as a deer in the forest, telling herself that if he'd wanted to hurt her, he could have done it when he'd first bounded out of his prison. Yet her pulse pounded in her ears, making her lightheaded.

The man of steel had a surprisingly gentle touch when he wanted it. Still, she stiffened as he grazed her blond hair with his free hand, murmuring something unintelligible.

The brush of his fingertips on her neck sent a shiver down her spine. Or perhaps it was the way his blue eyes skimmed each of her features as if committing them to memory. Tension crackled between them.

They might not be able to understand each other's language, but they were communicating on a level that hardly required words.

His tight focus on her was arresting, almost mesmerizing. He made another low comment as his fingers skimmed her cheek, her nose. When they reached her lips, she closed her eyes and swayed toward him, acknowledging some deep, primal level of connection between them. Then she blinked and pulled back sharply, astonished that she had permitted that kind of intimacy.

Perhaps he uttered an apology. She was in no position to know. She didn't breathe when his hand dropped to her shoulder and traced the open front of her bright pink parka, handling the soft fabric with the same concentration that he'd given her hair.

He asked another one of his questions—probably whether she'd gotten it at Bloomingdales or Saks.

''Neither. It's from Hudson Outfitters,'' she answered gravely.

He laughed, a rumble from deep in his chest.

Her gaze flew to his. Had he understood her joke? Then she realized he was simply responding to the terrible absurdity of the situation. The laugh transformed his face. Until now, his expression had wavered between grim and grave. Her heart gave a little lurch as she caught the promise of warmth. And an undefinable charm that made her insides melt. To cover her confusion, she put her hand to her mouth and gave a little cough. But she sensed that he wasn't fooled.

However, the laugh had a more practical effect, as well. It freed her from her trance. Her brain began to function on a more normal level, and she decided she was tired of having him control the situation. Especially when he could be arrested for indecent exposure.

"I wish you'd put something on," she said. She took off her jacket, disregarding its size, and thrust it toward him.

He looked at the garment, unmoving. Then, releasing her hand, he turned and strode toward a row of doors along the wall. Behind the first was a room made entirely of some low-luster metal. But she couldn't tell its function.

He left the door ajar and tried several others, all of which appeared to enclose supply cabinets. From the third, he pulled out a white lab coat of a slightly odd design, shook it open and slipped his arms nonchalantly through the sleeves. Then he closed the opening with what looked like a Velcro strip.

"Thanks. I guess you could tell all that tanned skin and rippling muscles were making me nervous," Cassie quipped in a conversational tone. At least there was one advantage to her situation. She could make any damn smart comment she wanted.

He answered in the language she didn't understand. Maybe with his own sarcastic rejoinder.

She couldn't take more of this. Seized by an overwhelming need to reach him on some meaningful level, she thumped her chest. "My name is Cassie. Cassie Devereaux. Maybe we can start with that."

He raised an eyebrow.

She realized she'd said too much. "I'm Cassie," she repeated and pointed to herself again. "Cassie."

"Cassie?"

On his lips, the syllables were warm and richly exotic.

She nodded.

He tried it out again, looking pleased. "Cassie Devereaux."

"Yes. And you?" She pointed toward him.

He hesitated for a moment. "Thorn."

"Thorn what?"

"Thorn."

"All right," she conceded. "It's just Thorn."

"ALL RIGHT. It's just Thorn," he parroted back. He had no understanding of what he was saying. Except for his name, he thought with frustration. He was a trained linguist, but he didn't know what tongue she was trying to teach him. It didn't have any root he could identify, but at least shades of meaning didn't seem to depend on guttural clicks. The stresses were unusual, however, and he was having trouble wrapping his mouth around the unfamiliar *j* sounds. And the grammar eluded him.

Cassie was waiting. Watching. For an unguarded moment, he wanted to touch her again, feel the incredible softness of her cheek, her lips, lose himself in the honesty of physical sensations.

As he focused on her face, he had the strong conviction he'd met her before. Or had he only dreamed of her? When he tried to analyze the thought, it evaporated like mist from the surface of a deep mountain lake.

He didn't know who she was. Or where she'd come from. Or exactly where they were playing out this drama. And when.

The last observation sent an icy chill sweeping across his skin. Panic threatened to engulf him. Underlying it was a profound sadness. He stifled both emotions with the force of his will.

The woman's eyes continued to question him. Before he started shouting out answers, he turned and strode toward the grooming alcove. Stepping across the threshold, he slammed the barrier behind him, hoping the mores of her culture would respect his privacy. After using the facilities, he leaned over the washing basin and splashed cold water on his face. His reflection in the three-dimensional mirror mocked him.

He looked sick.

That was the cue for a wave of nausea to rise in his throat. Swaying over the basin, he grasped the cold metal and retched up stomach acid. Grimacing, he opened a compartment and pulled out a tube of mouth refresher.

The spicy flavor swept away the nasty taste and made him feel a little better, but he knew the reprieve might be temporary. He'd been running on adrenaline, reacting from moment to moment since he stepped out of the delta cylinder—and his energy reserves were just about drained.

Dizzy, Thorn gripped the edge of the basin and forced himself to recall his last memories. They were from yesterday evening. Lodar and Darnot arriving at his quarters to continue the argument they'd been having for weeks. He remembered the older man coming up behind him and then a stinging sensation in his shoulder. The rest was a blur. Except for the part where Lodar was leaning over him, his face very close—telling him he was going to get what he deserved.

A cold sweat beaded his forehead. He risked another look in the mirror and saw his skin was the color of moldy mush.

It was the symptom his fuzzy brain had been unconsciously searching for. His system was going into a toxic reaction to the delta capsule. He'd seen it happen a couple of times after inadequate preparation. If he didn't get some ribenazine in the next few minutes, he was going to be on the floor, kicking and screaming and wishing he were dead. He wouldn't have long to wait. The next phases were irreversible coma and death.

As he lurched out of the grooming alcove, the woman looked at him in alarm and asked an urgent question he couldn't comprehend.

Sparing her a quick arm gesture, he commanded himself to stay conscious a few minutes longer as he staggered across the room to the cabinet marked with the symbol for healing. Inside he rummaged through small vials of liquid until his fingers closed around the one he needed. With fingers that felt thick and clumsy, he pulled at the seal. Too late. His formidable will lost the battle with his body and he crumpled to the floor.

Chapter Two

In seconds Cassie was across the room and kneeling beside him.

"Thorn!"

He didn't answer.

She looked from him to the cupboard. It was filled with small bottles and boxes of various sizes, none of which was familiar.

Frantically she knelt beside him and turned him on his back.

He'd looked ill.... Perhaps he'd been after some medication. But as far as she could see, he'd passed out before he could take anything.

The greenish cast of his skin was frightening. When she touched him, she found his flesh cold and clammy. The pulse in his neck was thready, his breathing labored. And a few minutes ago she'd heard him retching. He needed a doctor, but she was the only help he was going to get.

She'd seen him grab up a small bottle just before he lost consciousness. Lifting his hand, she pried the stiff fingers open and removed a vial of blue liquid. Would the contents cure him? Or kill him?

She shuddered as another disturbing thought struck

her. Was this a sudden attack of some *contagious* illness? Was that why he'd been isolated in this place?

Willing the ungenerous questions out of her mind, she concentrated on Thorn. How was she supposed to know what to do for him?

He'd been lying quietly on the stone floor. All at once his face contorted in pain, and he thrashed his arms and legs like a drowning man. Cassie grimaced at the agony etched into his features.

He cried out—two distinct words she didn't understand, repeating them several times. "Reah. Januk."

Then the thrashing grew more violent, racking him with frightening spasms that looked as if they would tear muscles and tendons.

"What should I do?" she begged.

Agony contorted his features. The spasms came hard and fast, one barely ending before the next one began.

His body wrenched, lifting him momentarily off the floor. He screamed, and his heels drummed. It was getting worse. Cassie sensed that whatever was wrong was going to kill him in a matter of minutes.

Swiftly making a decision, she pulled the seal off the bottle he'd been holding. Prying his jaw open with one hand, she tipped the vial to his lips with the other.

With agonizing slowness, the liquid dribbled into his mouth. He grimaced.

"Swallow it. Please swallow it." She waited tensely, all her senses tuned toward Thorn. Finally, he did.

"Thank you," she breathed. Now she could only wait and watch for some sign that she'd done the right thing.

His body still shook with spasms. Aching to do

something more to help him—anything—she pressed her torso against his and held his arms at his sides, trying to make sure that he didn't hurt himself. Although he was the patient and she the care giver, the physical contact was strangely comforting. Groping for his hands, she laced her fingers with his, and lay with her eyes closed, willing the viscous liquid to do its work.

She didn't know him, nor could she fathom what he was doing in this strange place. She couldn't even hold a meaningful conversation with him, for heaven's sake. But she felt that some kind of inexplicable bond had formed between them. At least that was the only way she could explain the terror that had overwhelmed her when he'd fallen to the floor.

By slow degrees she realized that the spasms were quieting, and the beat of his heart was growing stronger and more regular. For several more heartbeats, she kept her cheek pressed against his powerful chest. Then she raised her head. The agony on his face was only a shadow of remembered pain.

Cassie hovered over him, one of his large hands still clenched in hers. Finally he sighed and lay quiet like a swimmer who had finally pulled himself onto shore after a long, exhausting race.

"Thank God," she murmured.

His lids fluttered. His lips moved. And she sensed that he was making a tremendous effort to struggle toward consciousness. Hardly daring to breathe, she watched his face. His lids opened, and those startling blue eyes focused on her. Almost immediately, they registered surprise, then the same vulnerability she'd seen when he first came out of the transparent chamber.

"You're going to be fine," she told him, hoping her voice conveyed her meaning.

He tried to say something.

"No. You're too weak. Just sleep," she murmured. "We'll talk later."

Somehow.

His lids drifted closed. After a few moments, he appeared to sink into a normal sleep. She found blankets of some synthetic material in the supply cabinet and made him a bed.

Then, with an unsettled feeling, she looked down at him. What was it about this stranger that brought out such tender feelings? Usually she kept men at a distance. She'd learned not to get involved because she knew that the minute you let someone get close, you gave them the power to hurt you.

This was only a response to a fellow human being in need, she told herself. But she didn't really believe that. And the admission was frightening.

Silently, she backed away from Thorn. Now that the emergency was over, she'd better find a way out of this place. Behind the capsule where he'd first been standing were the computers she'd seen when she'd first entered the facility. She squinted at the equipment. The design was sleek and streamlined, obviously highly advanced models, but she'd used a variety of computers—both at the State Department and at the travel agency. Perhaps she could boot one of these. If it was connected to a modem, escape from this place could be as simple as a phone call.

Sitting down in a gray contour chair, she stared at the machine. There was a flat, glassy-looking screen embedded in a raised panel, but no keyboard. Was the system voice activated?

"Computer," she called out the way the crew did on the starship *Enterprise.*

Nothing happened, and she felt ridiculous. Maybe the keyboard would light up if she touched the desk.

The moment her hand connected with the machine, a bolt of electricity shot from the surface. It crackled over her skin and zinged like a burst of lightning through her whole body, making her gasp in pain.

Slumping in the chair, she cradled her hand against her chest. After several moments, she was left feeling weak and shaky. Holding out her hand, she stared from her reddened flesh to the desk and back again. So much for communicating with the outside world. She wasn't going to risk a shock like that again.

The hair on the top of her head prickled as if a secret door had opened to the underworld, and a cold breeze was blowing toward her. Until now, she'd thought of this installation as odd. Strange. A mystery as intriguing as its naked occupant. But the situation had taken another twist. She'd just learned that this hidden place was dangerous as well as strange. And perhaps deadly.

HALFWAY AROUND the world, Zeke Chambers leaned back in his rickety chair and finished the last of the strong, sweet coffee. His gray eyes scanned the view of unspoiled mountains against a crystal blue sky. The peaceful scene was deceiving. Yesterday at sunset, a small homemade bomb had ripped through the entrance to the cave his international team was excavating, turning the orderly dig site into chaos. Luckily, no one had died, and the structural damage was minimal. But two workers had been sent to the local physician, and the team's schedule was set back several days until the debris could be cleared.

Like the rest of his colleagues, Zeke had a tent at the site. But last night he'd slept in a real—if somewhat lumpy—bed in the village inn and treated himself to a hot shower. From his table at an outdoor café, he could see men and women making their way with carts and baskets to the market down the street where horse-drawn wagons full of vegetables and wares competed with small European cars for the parking spots along the main street. Had one of the innocent-looking villagers been responsible for the bombing? And why?

Zeke sighed. When Victor Kirkland at the State Department had helped him get this "plum assignment," the man had neglected to mention it might also be dangerous.

"Zesto café?" a young waitress interrupted his thoughts.

"No, I'm fine," he answered in her language.

Zeke popped a last bite of nut-and-cinnamon pastry into his mouth and wiped his sticky fingers on a cloth napkin before turning back to his laptop computer.

He could afford his own top-of-the-line equipment. In fact, the trust fund he'd come into three years ago when he'd turned thirty provided enough income for him to take any job he wanted—or not work at all if he chose. After an extended sabbatical last year, he'd found he was as happy backpacking through Europe as teaching anthropological linguistics at Johns Hopkins University in Baltimore.

With the hunt-and-peck style he'd developed to accommodate the dozens of foreign-language keyboards and word-processing programs he had to use, Zeke keyed in a few more lines to his log entry from the day before.

"Explosion at cave site under investigation. Could be local protestors who think we're going to cart off their national treasures. Or grave robbers trying to beat us to the punch. Should resume work by tomorrow afternoon."

"Good morning, Professor Chambers. May I join you?" a deferential voice inquired.

Zeke glanced up to see Dr. Feydor Lenov standing beside the table. The bearded Russian archeologist, a late addition to the team, had flown in several days before.

"Have a seat." Zeke saved his file, then popped the black disk from the laptop onto the tablecloth.

The Russian heaved his considerable bulk into a chair, and Zeke waited to see if it would take his weight. It did. He'd heard the man had been a competitive weight lifter in his youth.

After ordering coffee, Lenov leaned across the table and lowered his voice. "Heard anything more about the bombing?"

"Not much, except we can get back to work tomorrow."

"Well, I should hope so. I didn't come here to twiddle my thumbs. Montague will be hopping mad about the delay."

Zeke raised an eyebrow. "You've met our sponsor?"

"Once, several years ago at an exhibit in Paris, we exchanged a few words. He likes antiquities better than people." Lenov's accent sounded midwestern.

Zeke wondered if he'd learned his English in the

States or in a KGB training class. "Looking for something particular at the site?"

The Russian's answer was drowned out by the sound of an altercation at a neighboring table. Scraping his chair on the stone floor, he moved closer to Zeke and away from the ruckus.

The men who'd been arguing suddenly began trading punches. A table overturned, and customers scattered like frightened mice. Zeke grabbed his computer and jumped out of the way. For a large man, Lenov moved just as fast, dodging as one of the combatants fell across their table. With an angry look, the fighter pulled himself up. But his assailant had hightailed it down the street. Shouting insults, the injured party followed.

Zeke shook his head. His wonder at the volatile local temperament turned to paranoia as he righted the table and searched the floor. His disk had vanished.

AS CASSIE CRADLED her injured hand in her lap, she swiveled her chair toward the door where she'd entered. It was still wide open. For a wild moment she pictured herself dashing down the tunnel and into the cave of snow. She wanted to get away from this place. More than that, she wanted to get away from the man sleeping on the floor before he woke up and something else happened.

What?

She'd never felt so off balance. Or so open to possibilities. The combination left her feeling breathless. Yet escape was not an option. She'd simply be right back where she'd started a few hours ago. Trapped under an avalanche.

So whether she liked it or not, she was going to have to stay here and cope. With the mysterious environment. With its even more mysterious occupant. Thorn.

Cassie licked her dry lips. Was he the enemy?

All at once she remembered a weird situation she'd walked into back in college. She'd been in the almost-empty library during Christmas vacation because she was trying to get an extra-credit paper finished. Two male students had come up to the soda machine while she was taking a break. One was wearing scruffy jeans and a T-shirt with holes. The other sported an expensive sweater and stone-washed Calvins.

After they left, a guy who'd been watching from the corner sidled up and started asking a bunch of questions about which of the previous pair she thought was more likely to succeed in college.

She'd thought the questions odd and started to leave. He'd begged her to help him out because he was doing an experiment for a psychology class on women's expectations of men based on their clothing. Cassie had gotten away as quickly as she could.

In a lot of ways, this setup felt similar. She could almost imagine a team of scientists watching the action on television and scoring her responses on a scale from one to ten. How would she react to the naked man? What would she do when she discovered they couldn't communicate? What about when it looked as if he was dying?

Cassie sat up straighter. "Okay. I've figured it out. The experiment's over," she said to the room. "You can let me go home."

No speaker crackled to life. No doors opened, and her mouth firmed in disappointment. It was followed at once by an ironic little laugh. She hadn't really expected a response, had she? She hoped she wasn't that far gone.

This wasn't a case of getting trapped in the college library by a dorky grad student trawling for victims. She'd been caught in an avalanche and almost died. Her guide was probably under a ton of snow.

And there was one more factor she'd been trying not to think about. Her own compulsion to come here. She shivered. She'd pulled strings to get this assignment—fought for it in ways that were completely out of character for her. And ever since she'd arrived, she'd had a sense she was fulfilling a destiny written in the stars long ago.

Nonsense, she told herself.

Standing too quickly, she reached to steady herself against the desk. At the last second she cursed and pulled her hand from harm's way, taking a step back.

Automatically she glanced at Thorn to see if he'd heard. Then she cursed again at the double stupidity. He was out cold. Even if he could hear, he wouldn't understand.

She grimaced. Every way she twisted and turned in this bizarre place, she came up against a new problem. She didn't like having no control. And she didn't like waiting for someone to wake up and tell her which machines were safe to touch. Particularly a man. Her father had made damn sure of that.

Unable to stand still while her mind spun in circles, Cassie stomped toward the room where Thorn had closeted himself before rushing to grab the medicine bottle. She'd heard water running while he was inside. Odds were it was a kitchen or a bathroom.

But after crossing the threshold, she stopped short.

It took a moment to orient herself. There was a funnel-shaped object coming out of the floor. A toilet? She peered into the hole. No water. And no flushing mechanism.

What might be a sink was a shallow trough jutting out of the wall. Then she caught a glance at her reflection in the mirror above it. Instead of being flat, the image was three-dimensional.

She stood very still and pressed her fingers against the surface. It felt hard and flat. Yet the rectangle displayed her head and shoulders as if she were looking at a brilliantly clear holographic image. Eyes wide, she swung from side to side, noting that she could practically see the back of her head—as well as every imperfection in her skin.

Who would go to the trouble of using advanced holographic technology on a bathroom mirror, Cassie wondered as she gazed at the startling image.

With a shrug she looked for water taps. There were none. But when she brought her hand over the trough, water sprayed from hidden nozzles in the wall. It was warm. With a little experimentation, she found that by bringing her hand closer to the wall or moving it farther away, she could adjust the temperature.

What looked like decorative columns above the sink turned out to be two stacks of lightweight tumblers fitted into grooves in the wall. Cassie filled a glass and took a cautious sip. To her pleasure, the water tasted as if it had come from a crystal-clear mountain stream. Well, at least that was something.

"So who designed this place?" she asked her unconscious companion as she emerged again. "Is the Defense Department using it to test advanced technologies? Are you training for an invasion of Mars?

Or is this like in World War II when they used Native American languages as a communications code? Is that your background?''

She looked inquiringly at the slant of his closed eyes and the copper color of his skin. ''No answers? What a surprise.''

However, he stirred restlessly in his sleep, his mouth drawn as if in pain.

Instantly she was contrite. He wasn't responsible for what had happened to her. In fact, he'd seemed as confounded by the situation as she. ''I'm sorry. I didn't mean to disturb you.'' Kneeling beside him, she smoothed back the straight black hair that had fallen across his forehead. Not a military haircut, she noted absently as she fingered the strands. They were surprisingly silky.

She should stop touching him. Yet she craved the contact. It was because they were trapped here together, she told herself. Because he was the only other person in this alien place and they needed each other to survive. Yet she knew that didn't fully explain the tightness in her throat. The worry. The fear of loss. She felt those things for this man called Thorn, whether she admitted it or not.

Her gaze took in more details. His lashes were even darker than his hair. His features spoke of maturity, yet his skin was almost unlined, except around his eyes. Awake, he'd been forceful, antagonistic, even harsh. Sleeping, he looked peaceful. And defenseless. She couldn't stop herself from gently touching his lips. They moved against her fingers, responding to the intimate contact, and the movement sent a little shiver up her arm.

Cassie pulled her hand away, yet she didn't want

to sever the human contact. Flattening her fingers against his chest, she felt his heartbeat once more. The rhythm was sure and steady. His breathing was normal. Abandoning medical observations, she slipped inside the front closing of his coat and stroked her fingers through the thick hair of his chest.

"You're in trouble, aren't you?" she whispered. "We're both in trouble. Are you going to tell me about it?"

Cassie hardly expected an answer. She certainly didn't expect Thorn's hand to cover hers. But it did. Her gaze shot to his face. His blue eyes were open, and he was staring at her with a look of mingled wonder and wariness.

THORN REMEMBERED every detail of the few minutes he'd spent with this woman—starting with the moment he'd stepped out of the delta capsule.

Things had happened quickly. Too quickly. Ending with long, agonizing seconds when he'd known he was going to die, and he'd called out to the two people who mattered most to him. His heart squeezed painfully, and he pushed their images away. If he started thinking about what might have happened to Reah and Januk, he'd go insane.

So he focused every particle of his attention on the woman who crouched over him. She'd saved his life by getting the ribenazine into him.

Why? Had she been acting under Lodar's instructions to make the captive drop his defenses by saving his life? Perhaps he was being too cynical.

Whatever her goal, he sensed the tension radiating from her in almost palpable waves. Of course, she had good reason to be afraid. Of him. Of this place.

Either she was playing a very dangerous game or she'd stumbled into a situation completely beyond her ken.

He sat up and leaned against the supply cabinet, wincing at the stab of pain that felt like a nail being driven into his forehead. When he tried to get to his feet, the woman put a restraining hand on his shoulder.

"No."

It wasn't difficult to guess the meaning of the short syllable she uttered. It was more than a polite suggestion—it was an order.

With an inward sigh, he conceded the point. Relaxing as best he could, he looked at her inquiringly. She met his gaze steadily, a bold move for a native woman. If that's what she was.

He studied her face. She was very beautiful, with gently wavy hair the color of warm light cast by an oil lamp. It went well with the alabaster skin that bloomed with a hint of pink over her high cheekbones in response to his scrutiny. His gaze was drawn to her clear emerald eyes that at first glance seemed a little too large. They were just the opposite of her nose. It was small and delicate and entirely feminine. As feminine as the gentle curve of her mouth. He'd never seen anyone like her before. Anywhere.

He took the hand from his shoulder and looked at the back. Her fingers were long, tapered, smooth—and strong, he added, remembering her grip on his jaw when she'd been trying to get the medicine into him. Her nails were rounded and buffed. No, he amended as he smoothed his thumb across their surface. They were coated with a shiny, transparent substance he'd never seen before.

She shivered under his touch, but didn't draw away or lower her eyes.

"Ah, you are very bold, Cassie," he said in his own tongue, wishing she could grasp his meaning, wishing he could gauge her reaction.

She responded to her name with a tiny twitch of her lips. He pushed her a little further, shifting his grip to find her pulse. The beats accelerated.

She remained very still, trying wordlessly to convey the impression that she wasn't afraid of him. He knew from her shallow breathing and her pounding heart that it was a lie. Yet he kept coming back to the central truth of their short acquaintance. She'd saved his life when she could have left him convulsing on the floor.

He'd give a lot to know her real motives. Since he could hardly conduct an interrogation, he cataloged other observations. He could tell a lot from her hand, for example. And from the way she took care of her hair and face. She looked no more than twenty. Yet she was wise beyond those years. She was from the ruling class. Perhaps even royalty, because she'd never done manual labor. She was from a land far away from the one where he'd been assigned, since she hadn't been raised to defer to his people. In fact, she seemed to have no idea of his status.

He turned her hand over and saw a red circle on her index finger that looked like a recent burn.

When he gave it the barest touch, she winced.

"What happened?" he asked in his own language, accompanying the question with a raised eyebrow that he hoped would help convey his meaning.

She caught on immediately. Scrambling up, she crossed the room and pointed to one of the data analyzer terminals, waving her arms and spouting a long string of words that meant nothing. When he looked perplexed, she strode into the grooming alcove and emerged with one of the drinking goblets.

Was she going to pour water on the delicate equipment? That was all he needed.

''No,'' he ordered, using one of the few words he'd learned of her language.

Ignoring him, she tossed the vessel at the machine and jumped back. When the missile hit, an electrical discharge sizzled like a bolt of lightning.

''Klat!'' The curse was wrung from him in anger—and surprise. ''That is how you got burned?'' he asked in his own tongue, frustrated that he couldn't get an answer. What he wouldn't give for a language decoder.

She responded with a sigh and a question of her own, part words, part pantomime. She pointed to him, pretended to touch the equipment and made a sound like an explosion, ''Boom!''

It was accompanied by appropriate hand gestures, the performance very telling. She was asking if the same thing would happen to him.

He shrugged. ''Ask Lodar.'' Even as he made the suggestion, he felt a mixture of anger and apprehension stir inside him. Teeth clamped together, he pushed himself off the floor and discovered his muscles felt like pudding. Before he'd taken two shaky steps, Cassie was at his side, holding him back. He was chagrined to discover that at the moment she had more strength than he. Obviously he was in worse shape than he'd realized.

He saw her eyes were round with worry. That, as much as her restraining hands, stopped him from crossing the room. He wasn't used to anyone caring so passionately about what happened to him. Bemused, he reversed his course. But before sitting down on the makeshift bed, he found a packet of regenerating salve in the healing cabinet.

"Come here," he said quietly, accompanying the order with a hand gesture.

Hesitantly she sat beside him.

"Let me fix your hand." Although she couldn't understand, it was strangely calming to simply talk to her.

He opened the packet of salve and rubbed a little on the back of his own hand to show her it was all right. Then he reached for hers. Careful of the burned flesh, he spread the ointment on her wound.

He saw her draw in a quick breath. Saw her let it out in a soft sigh as the salve began to soothe.

She stared down at her injured skin, watching the red color fade. Then she raised wide, questioning eyes to his.

He shrugged and squeezed her fingers. For long moments, she sat with her hand in his. They couldn't talk, yet words were hardly necessary now. He was content to be simply with her like this for hours, the innocent contact like a healing balm. Languid warmth stole over him.

She started to lean on his shoulder. Then her head jerked up, and the rosy flush he liked so much spread across her cheeks. So she'd felt the closeness, too. And it made her skittish.

She blinked, her face changing from guileless to guarded. Scrambling up, she darted across the room, picked up a blue carry bag and brought it over. When she returned, she sat an arm's length from him and began to rummage inside. With a little grin, she pulled out a small leather-covered book and what looked like a writing instrument. Fascinated, he waited to find out what she had in mind—besides putting some distance between them.

She opened the book and passed it to him. The pages were covered with unintelligible symbols. The only things he knew for sure was that her people had a well-developed written language that used an alphabet rather than ideograms. And that her handwriting was precise.

He shrugged.

She found an unused sheet and drew two people. One had a parody of his face. The other had longer hair and two half circles to indicate breasts. She pointed to the first one. "Thorn."

He beat her to the punch and pointed to the other. "Cassie."

She nodded, obviously pleased. Underneath, she carefully wrote a string of the symbols he'd seen on the previous pages.

"Cassie," she pronounced as he studied the configuration, noting double consonant in the middle.

When he pointed to each symbol, she gave him the phonetic sound. "Kaa-see." They repeated the process for Thorn.

He sighed. In a couple of weeks, they might get somewhere with this. By that time they might both be dead.

She pointed to him and grimaced, her face showing pain, her shoulders sagging in weariness. She used a word he'd heard her say just before he'd fallen asleep. "Thorn weak."

"Weak," he repeated in her language, wishing he

could pretend he hadn't comprehended the meaning. *Sick and vulnerable. Lacking strength.* They were probably all good approximations. He scowled at her.

She looked apologetic, as if she knew how much he hated the observation. A timid woman would have backed off. Instead, she followed with a drawing of the Thorn figure lying on a bed, his eyes closed. "Thorn...needs...sleep."

The next picture showed Thorn standing straight and tall. She drew him again, sitting at the analyzer and walking through a door. Pausing, she took her lip between her teeth. Then at the top of the page she drew a circle with wavy lines radiating from the perimeter.

He studied the sketch, and his chest tightened as he deciphered the pictogram. She'd drawn an almost universal symbol—a sun. He pointed toward the sky, tipped his face up and closed his eyes, pretending to bask in pleasant warmth.

She nodded eagerly. "Sun," she supplied and began speaking rapidly.

He put up a hand to stop her. He didn't know the meaning of the words flowing from her, but he understood she thought he'd be smart to get some sleep before exploring this place. With a sigh, he crossed his legs at the ankles and inclined his head toward the cabinet of healing supplies. Inside were several varieties of cutaneous patches he could use. One would put him into a deep, mending sleep for several hours. The prospect was tempting. If he'd been alone, he wouldn't have hesitated to use it. But he couldn't risk being out of commission while his companion's motives were still in doubt.

Her green eyes regarded him solemnly. This time

he was the one who broke the contact. He longed to trust her. Longed to give in to the conviction that they were in this together. But he'd be a fool to act from such weakness. He looked toward the cabinet again.

A different patch would put his system in overdrive. But he couldn't go that route, either, since the dose had to be strictly rationed. If he took a stimulant jolt now, he wouldn't have the option of using it later when he might need it more.

Thorn sighed. He'd find out soon enough what nasty surprises Lodar had left for him. For all he knew, there might even be an army outside, waiting patiently for him to stick his head out the door. Unfortunately, he was in no shape to take them on yet.

Or maybe his present problems had nothing to do with the man he'd been foolish enough to provoke. Maybe the installation where he'd awakened was simply falling apart.

Because? An answer popped into his mind. He felt the walls closing in on him, and for several heartbeats he fought sheer, blinding terror. Then he drew on the inner reserves that had gotten him this far. There was no use getting worked up about how bad his situation *might* be.

His thoughts retreated to a safer venue. He'd take Cassie's advice—because it was the smartest course. For tonight the best thing to do was concentrate on getting his strength back. And while he was at it, he'd see what he could tease out of this woman who was so warm and close with him one moment and so skittish the next.

Chapter Three

Zeke roared down a gravel road on his rented Harley-Davidson. The countryside sped by in a blur of dark green trees, pink and yellow wildflowers and gray rocky hills. But his mind wasn't on the scenery. This morning, after the incident with the stolen disk, he'd nosed around the café and the market trying to get a lead on the men who'd started the fight. Either they were outsiders, or the locals weren't talking.

After steering the powerful bike off the road onto a rutted dirt path, he had to slow his speed to dodge a pothole that would have swallowed a tank. Around the next bend, he came to a sun-dappled clearing dominated by a mammoth granite boulder. For more than a thousand years, it had covered the mouth of a limestone cave. But infrared satellite analysis had yielded the secret of the interior, and reclusive billionaire Jacques Montague had quickly put together a team to explore the site.

A dozen small tents surrounded a large one that served as both dining hall and artifact repository. The living conditions in camp were Spartan, not that much different from a dozen other underfunded sites Zeke had worked. But Montague had supplied some pretty sophisticated equipment—everything from heavy construction machinery to a portable cellular communications system. There were all sorts of rumors about the man. According to one, he had a terminal illness and was determined to find something as important as the Dead Sea Scrolls before he died. Even Victor Kirkland from the State Department had only sketchy information about their eccentric sponsor.

The dig was usually bustling with activity. Today, it was quiet since few of the dig team had gotten back from town. Marie Pindel, the team leader, was hurrying toward the cave.

Zeke pulled up beside her and cut the engine.

She gave him a startled look. With her cap of dyed copper hair and large eyes, the petite Frenchwoman looked more like a fashion model in her designer jeans and knit top than a forty-seven-year-old anthropologist with two controversial best-sellers and three grandchildren to her credit.

"I didn't expect you back so soon," she said. "I was just going over to survey the damage. The local police have finally packed up their little meters and magnifying glasses and decided we won't embarrass them by dying of carbon monoxide poisoning." She shrugged expressively. "As if we didn't have equipment ten times as sensitive as theirs."

Zeke unsnapped his helmet. "You're breaking your own rule about going in alone?"

"I won't have to, now that you're here. Let's go take a look," she called over her shoulder as she took off again.

Grabbing his tool pack from the motorcycle's carry case, Zeke trotted after her to the cave entrance. As always, it was a tight squeeze through the narrow opening for his six-foot-three, one-hundred-ninety-pound frame, and he had to take it sideways all the way to the main chamber where they'd been working. While Marie adjusted the battery lantern and checked the air quality, Zeke trained a high-powered flashlight on the damage from the homemade bomb.

He grimaced as the beam played over the stone walls in the far corner of the gallery where only two days before he'd been transcribing picture script. Now much of the stone engraving had been obliterated by the blast. But that wasn't the worst. A burial pit, which had yielded a decorative vase, a curved plow called a crook ard and several smaller tools forged from iron had evidently taken the brunt of the explosive. It was now black ash and rubble.

Marie's eyes flashed with anger. "How could anyone do such a thing?"

"Who knows?" Zeke muttered. "At least we rescued some of the artifacts before the blast. And I'll be able to work with the low light exposures of the wall script and the notes I've transcribed." Disgustedly, he stepped closer to the scarred stone. The light beam caught on a crack that ran from floor to ceiling. Had the explosion caused that, too?

Starting at the bottom and moving upward, he felt along the break. It seemed solid. Relieved, he stepped back and inspected the surface again. The beam played down the limestone and up again, illuminating a strange mark a good foot above his head. At first, he thought it was residue from the blast. On closer inspection, he could almost make out a faint imprint.

"Qu'est-ce que c'est?" Marie asked.

"I don't know." Stretching, he pressed his palm

against it. The stone seemed to warm. They both gasped as the hard rock split along a six-foot seam to reveal a small room no bigger than a walk-in closet.

"My God!" Zeke exclaimed as the flashlight illuminated the space inside. A large, finely engraved bronze box sat on a pottery tile on the floor.

Marie was by his side in an instant. "The explosion must have broken the seal on a hidden tomb."

His pulse raced with excitement. Gently, as if working with the most delicate glass, he felt over the surface of the box until his fingers found a hidden latch. Inside were several perfectly preserved panels covered with writing.

"Well, I'll be damned!"

Marie leaned over his shoulder, shining the light directly on the script. "Can you tell what it is?"

Being careful not to touch the material, he studied the characters. One panel resembled ancient Greek script, yet it appeared to be another language altogether. There was a picture, too. A naked man in a strange-looking capsule.

Tentatively he touched the surface. "This doesn't make sense," he told Marie. "Feel the covering. It's almost like plastic."

She touched the panel and nodded. "As far as I know, no one from the ninth century B.C. had anything like this. You think it's a fake?" she asked.

"Do you?"

"I want you to check it out before we tell the others. We might be sitting on the most important discovery since the Dead Sea Scrolls. Or..."

"Someone could be playing a very nasty joke," she finished for him.

To her embarrassment, Cassie's stomach growled.

Thorn said something in his own language and made eating motions.

She nodded. "I suppose there's a kitchen somewhere around here," she said in an artificially chipper tone. "But it may not have anything I'd recognize as a stove. And even if you're willing to do the cooking, the equipment could explode in your face when you touch the controls. So why don't I dig into my emergency supplies?"

Thorn leaned back and watched her, apparently very interested in what she intended to do.

The scrutiny made her feel self-conscious, and she lowered her eyes. She was coming to realize that in the confines of this room, the simplest actions had monumental meaning. Each thing she and Thorn experienced together was fresh and new. An adventure. A clue to understand each other. And more. A strand of the growing bond tying them to each other. Part of her was wary. The way she'd always been. Part of her longed to get closer to this man.

Ducking her head, she pulled some packets of dehydrated soup from her knapsack and handed them to Thorn. He shook them, listened to the dry grains rattle inside and shrugged.

"Just add hot water and you've got a meal in a bowl," she announced, imitating a TV commercial. It was so much easier to make silly conversation he couldn't understand than to cope with the confusion she felt.

In the bathroom, she filled two cups with hot water. When she brought them back, she found Thorn had torn open one of the envelopes.

After sniffing the contents, he dipped a finger inside and cautiously brought a bit of the dry mix to his tongue.

He made a face, then looked on with interest as she added the mix to the water and stirred with a plastic spoon.

"Chicken soup," she informed him as she looked at her watch. "Good for what ails you."

He took her wrist and examined the timepiece as if he'd never seen anything like it. She pointed to the second hand, made a circle around the watch face and held up three fingers. "It'll be done in a jiffy."

Apparently more interested in the instrument than her scintillating commentary, he slipped the expansion band over her wrist.

After studying the face, he grabbed her pencil and notebook and copied the numbers from the dial to a clean sheet of paper, writing them in a line across the page.

As he pointed to each, she gave him the name. "One, two, three, four..." Up to twelve.

He held up his fists and began to raise one finger at a time, reciting, "One, two, three, four, five..."

"Yes!" she exclaimed.

He went through the ten fingers and examined his hands like a magician who's just made a coin disappear. "Eleven? Twelve?"

"Hmm," she mused. "I guess I never thought about it. Our number system is based on ten. But the day is divided into twenty-four hours."

Taking the pencil she drew a circle and bisected it. On the right she drew the sun; on the left, a crescent moon. Then she marked off twelve divisions on each side.

When she looked at Thorn expectantly he nodded and pointed to the numbers on the watch.

"Right. Twelve hours in a day." She tapped the sun. "And twelve hours in a night." She tapped the moon. "Give or take variations for summer and winter, of course."

His face was a study in concentration.

"Understand?" she asked.

"Understand," he repeated, nodding vigorously.

"Good."

Snatching up the notebook, he flipped back several pages to the third drawing she'd made. Thorn lying in bed. Eyes closed. "Thorn...sleep...night," he said slowly but distinctly.

A shiver went through her. He'd put together enough words to make a sentence in a language he'd never heard before today. Was he a genius or a trained linguist? "My God. Yes," she whispered.

He looked pleased with himself. And eager for more.

"Okay. Try this." She wrote, "2 + 2 = 4" and handed over the notebook.

He countered with "2 + 3 = 5."

For the first time since she'd bumbled into never-never land, Cassie forgot to worry about her predicament. Instead, she was totally focused on Thorn. It was as if a door had opened between them. She was reaching him on a new level of understanding, and she wanted to go even further.

Cassie had no idea how long they sat there, close together, going over more complex concepts. But she did realize that he hadn't taken his eyes off her; she felt her cheeks grow warm. For the last while he was looking at her differently, and she knew that in some subtle way his opinion of her had changed. She picked up her cup and took a swallow. Then she gestured toward Thorn's.

"Eat your chicken soup," she urged.

He nodded and sipped cautiously.

"Well? Good? Bad? Okay?" She accompanied each question with the appropriate facial expression.

"Chicken soup...okay." He took several more swallows. Then, putting his cup down, he held out his hands in front of him, about two feet apart. Sawing the right one up and down he said, "Good." For emphasis he imitated her previous smiling face. Then he repeated with "Bad."

She took another swallow as he turned the "good" hand up and slanted her what she'd come to think of as his questioning look. At the same time, he moved his fingers in a gesture that appeared to indicate that he wanted her to give him something. What did he want? Then it dawned on her that in any well-developed language, there should be a lot of words for such important concepts as good and bad.

His eyes seemed to darken as he reached out and took her hand, squeezing a little as if to encourage her.

His fingers were strong and warm. Her throat was suddenly dry as he shifted his grip to bring her palm in contact with his. She fought to keep from dropping her gaze or pulling away.

"Uh, nice..." That was much too tepid for what she was feeling. "Enjoyable...pleasurable...wonderful...sexy..."

Cassie flushed scarlet as she realized where the chain of associations had taken her. Her embarrassment increased as he solemnly gave her back the words. Damn his phenomenal memory. She could picture him congratulating her with a slap on the back and a hearty, "Sexy job."

More than that, she knew she'd given away too much. And it didn't help to tell herself that he hadn't understood the implications. He'd figure it out the way he was catching on to everything else.

She was about to pick up her cup when he slipped his hand under her chin and tipped her face toward his.

"I—" She didn't know what she was going to say because he drove the thought completely out of her mind by stroking her jaw line. Her breath caught in her throat when his finger moved to her lips.

"Thorn..."

"Pleasurable...wonderful...sexy," he pronounced, giving the words deeper meaning.

"Yes." She sat very still as his fingers drifted to the side of her neck, feeling her pulse. It was already beating furiously. At his light touch, the tempo speeded up.

He held her gaze. Held her captive as surely as if he'd slipped a handcuff over her wrist and clicked the lock home. She forgot to breathe as his hand moved lower, brushing aside the front of her coat, gliding over the knit fabric of her shirt, over the swell of her breast. Her nipples tightened. And she knew he felt it. By the catch in his throat, by the way his blue eyes deepened.

He stroked her, murmuring something she couldn't understand—but his voice sent an erotic current shooting through her body. For a yearning moment she swayed toward him, yielding to the physical contact and something more elemental. Deep in her subconscious, she felt as if this kind of touching, this response, had happened between them before. That they were renewing a previous and very intimate acquaintance.

Then she caught herself. What was she doing? More to the point, what the hell was *he* doing?

"No!" She pulled away from him, her eyes shooting sparks that told him what she thought of his behavior. The nerve of the man—taking that kind of liberty. And where had she gotten the wacky idea that it was safe to drop her guard?

He said something that might have been an apology.

She glared at him. Yet deep inside she knew it wasn't all his fault. She should have stopped him.

But at what point? When he touched her jaw? Her lips? It was obvious he didn't know the rules of her society. Or maybe he didn't care.

Unwilling to look at him, she scooted away, putting several feet between them. She didn't trust him. Or herself now. And she felt so confused, she had to blink back tears. For thirty years she'd avoided involvements. A few hours with this man and she was breaking every rule she'd ever made. She wanted to get up and make camp on the other side of the room. Instead she settled for turning back to her soup, eating as if her life depended on it, while she tried to fathom her own out-of-character behavior.

He said nothing. Instead he ate slowly. Cassie finished and was thinking about fixing two more cups when a change in the background hum of the station made her lift her head and sit very still. Thorn was also listening intently.

She saw a puzzled expression flash across his face

just before the lights blinked. Then they went out, plunging the room into total blackness.

In the dark, she heard him bite out the word that she understood was a curse, *''Klat!''*

''What's happening?'' she asked in a shaky voice.

Thorn echoed the question in his own language. Reaching across the empty space separating him from Cassie, he found her arm and tugged her toward him. Her body went rigid. A clattering noise made *his* body tense for an attack. Then he realized her foot had hit an empty soup cup, sending it skittering across the floor.

He cursed again. He was jumpy as a bush stalker in heat. But why not, when he half expected armed men to come pelting into the room.

When Cassie tried to pull away from him, he gripped her shoulder. He understood why she might resist his touch. He knew full well he'd overstepped the bounds a few minutes ago when he'd cupped her breast, stroked her erect nipple. But when he'd felt her pulse quicken, he'd known it wasn't out of fear, and some arrogant male impulse had urged him to find out how far he could go with her—even as he'd told himself he was simply conducting a sociology experiment. How would a female in her culture respond to advances from a strange male?

She tried again to pull away, but he held her tightly, unwilling to let her vanish into the darkness. Was the station under attack from hostile forces? Had the life-support system been damaged? Or was this simply a routine maintenance sequence, scheduled for the middle of the night?

He listened intently, prepared for any possibility. Silence reigned around them. The only thing his keen senses could pick up was that the temperature had dropped a couple of degrees.

Cassie kept trying to wiggle out of his grasp, growing increasingly agitated as she repeated a message he couldn't decipher. ''No!'' he ordered in her language.

She answered with what sounded like a plea. ''Please.'' She'd used the word before, he recalled. When she'd been trying to get the medicine into him. He'd been near comatose, but his hearing had still been functioning. Was her present purpose equally urgent? A matter of life and death for both of them? Or had Lodar told her she'd better be at least ten feet from Thorn when the lights went out?

He sighed in the darkness, torn between paranoia and anger at himself. For the past hour he'd been seduced into a feeling of camaraderie with the very beautiful Cassie Devereaux. More than camaraderie, he admitted with a grimace. He'd been weak enough to fall under her spell. But he'd better remember that she could be the agent of his destruction.

The first order of business was to make sure she didn't slip away in the darkness, leaving him sitting with his back to the wall. He found her right hand and laced the fingers with hers.

''Okay,'' he muttered in her language, waiting to find out what she wanted to do.

Tentatively she leaned forward. He heard her carry sack slide toward them and wished he could see what she was doing as she fumbled with the contents. He was startled when she braced a cold, hard tube against their locked hands.

A weapon?

He snatched the cylinder out of her grasp. As his

hand slid along the barrel, a beam of light shot from the end of the tube, slicing a path through the darkness.

"Flashlight," she informed him.

He was glad she couldn't see his hot face. The thing was merely a light source. But how long would it last?

The room was getting colder. Cassie pulled her jacket closed. As if by mutual agreement, they stood.

Willing himself to steadiness, he led her across the room to the door where she'd presumably entered. Playing the light down the dark tunnel, he breathed a little sigh when it proved to be empty. At least they weren't being invaded. Yet. When he pressed the lock pad, there was no response.

"I need to check the main generator," he told her, wishing she could follow what he was saying.

Cassie hung back as they approached the data analyzers. He reassured her with calm words before shining the light on the partition beyond. She nodded tightly as they skirted the machines that had given her the shock.

Although his manner was brisk as he reached for the access panel, she tensed.

They both let out a little sigh when the door came open without incident. Using the light, he examined the station controls and the specification charts. He could see from the schematic that there were three solar-powered units attached to electrical storage grids. Two were completely drained from a recent malfunction. The third was operating a few essential systems—like air purification—and automatically conserving energy for an emergency. Perhaps the damage to the power units could even explain the shock she'd gotten.

He pointed to the schematic and indicated the power source. "Sun."

Cassie nodded vigorously, and he wondered if she really understood about solar collectors and electrical conversion.

He continued the explanation for himself, since he knew she couldn't possibly follow. "The solar collectors are rapid recovery units. Let's hope power is restored to something approaching normal when the sun comes out in the morning."

She seemed reassured by his even tones. Or maybe she'd simply observed that he wasn't dashing for an escape hatch.

He struggled to mask his frustration. It was one thing to play sexy little games with this woman. It was quite another to get some real answers out of her.

"How did you break in here? What is happening outside?" he demanded, wishing she could tell him what he needed to know as he pointed toward the door. Yet what did it matter what she said? He couldn't afford to trust her.

"I guess were going to have to take a look," he said in clipped tones, pulling her toward the door. They both shivered in the icy air wafting toward them.

"C-o-l-d," Cassie said in her own language, giving the observation teeth-chattering emphasis he had no trouble comprehending.

He repeated the temperature appraisal. "Cold." Next they'd be discussing the barometric pressure and the projected global weather forecast.

She darted back to the makeshift bed, retrieved a blanket and draped it over his shoulders. "Warm."

"Warm." Two brilliant new concepts, he congratulated himself, feeling ridiculous huddling under a shawl like an old woman. But he conceded the virtue of prudence. And dignity. If someone was waiting outside, he didn't want to greet them looking as if he'd tottered from a sickbed. Opening a supply cabinet, he began to search for something more substantial than a technician's coat. He was rewarded with a cache of silver knit pants and shirts—the expedition's standard issue.

When he threw off the blanket and started to unbutton the thin coat, she turned quickly away. He'd forgotten about her ridiculous nudity taboo.

Stomping into the grooming alcove, he shucked off the coat and pulled on the pants and shirt. He followed with a pair of thermal socks, wishing he could add boots.

When he came out, she nodded her approval.

He didn't want her approval. Ignoring her, he marched back to the entrance. Ice seemed to seep through the bottoms of his feet as he and Cassie made their way down the tunnel. The passage ended at a broken doorway that he could see had been camouflaged as rock.

When he started to shoulder through, Cassie said something that began with "Av—"

Ignoring her, he stepped through the ruined barrier. Almost immediately, he halted in surprise. He was in a long, narrow cave—so long that it swallowed up the flashlight beam. The wall from which he'd emerged was of dark rock. The facing one was made of snow.

So how had Cassie gotten in? He wasn't about to

let her start drawing pictures again. He wasn't going to trust anything besides his own observations. For a moment he stood, listening to the utter silence. Then, doggedly ignoring the cold, he made his way down the tunnel between the black rock and the white snow.

Cassie kept pace with him, talking all the while. When he ignored her, she grabbed his sleeve and yelled, *"Klat!"*

The curse got his attention. He stopped short and turned. She gave him an exasperated look.

After a moment, she repeated a word she'd used before. "Avalanche." First she pointed to the snow. Then rolling her hands in a circle, she swept them in a downward motion. Looking behind her, she pretended to run. Finally she put her arms over her head and huddled down, protecting herself from the onslaught.

"Avalanche," she said again. "Understand?"

"Avalanche," he repeated, finally picturing what had happened. Snow had come roaring down the mountain toward her, and she'd taken refuge against the rock face.

"Understand?" she asked again.

"Yes."

"Good."

It was their longest conversation. Too bad he was almost as articulate as an illiterate camel driver.

However, Cassie looked pleased. Taking a step back, she raised her arms and stretched, as if to dissipate some of her tension. Her hands slammed into the wall of white that hung over her.

Quickly she pulled them back. But the damage was already done. Recently settled snow began to tumble down on top of her so quickly that Thorn barely had time to gasp out a useless warning. One minute she was in front of him gesticulating. In the next, she had disappeared, buried under an enormous pile of freezing whiteness.

Chapter Four

A mixture of fear and astonishment wrenched through Thorn as he stared at the place where Cassie had been standing moments ago. His first reckless impulse was to toss the flashlight aside and start digging her out with both hands. Instead he clenched the cold metal tube. The blasted cave was pitch-dark; he needed to see what he was doing.

Using up a few precious seconds, he scraped together a little pile of snow and made a stand for the light so that the beam was positioned in the right direction.

There was no margin for error, he thought with a grimace as he started to dig with the only tools he had. Almost at once his fingers grew icy. He ignored the numbing pain and scraped away at the snow, alternately cursing himself, calling Cassie's name and gasping drafts of air into his lungs.

His whole body was shivering violently from the cold. No, more than the cold. His head spun. He knew he was in no shape for the unexpected exertion. But somehow he kept digging. Because he had to get the snow off of Cassie before she suffocated. So he continued to toss white clouds behind him as he worked in the semidarkness and to pray that he wouldn't be too late.

It seemed to take forever. It was probably less than a minute when he felt something harder than the recently settled snow. Not rock. Something that yielded to his touch, although with his hands numb from the cold, he couldn't tell much.

He saw the bright pink outerwear covering Cassie's back and gave silent thanks as he corrected the direction of his search. Redoubling his efforts, he scooped like a madman. His fingers slid off her shoulder. He dug lower and hooked his hand around her arms, giving a mighty tug. One arm came free. Immediately she began to dig, too, and he knew what he'd only sensed before. She didn't give up easily.

With a sigh of relief, he brushed the snow away from her nose and mouth. She shook her head and sucked in a gasp of air that ended with his name. Her face was white and etched with terror. Yet her eyes were focused squarely on him as if she couldn't believe that he'd gotten her out.

Remorse was a dagger stabbing into his heart.

He couldn't judge the coldness of her skin. His own hands were too numb. But he kept working as he told her she was safe. That she was going to be all right. That he was sorry. That he'd been a fool to come out here where she could get hurt. He wished she could understand some of it; he was glad she couldn't catch the rest.

Finally, she was able to push with her hands. The snow broke apart, and she tumbled out, knocking him over, exclaiming something that was probably thanks to her deity.

He repeated the words because he didn't know what else to say. "Thank God."

For an endless moment they both sprawled unmoving on the freshly scattered snow, breathing in great gasps of air. Then his arms came up to clasp her tightly, his hands shaking with emotion and cold. He'd almost gotten her killed—because he'd refused to trust her. And the only thing she'd done to provoke his suspicion was to stumble into the wrong place at the wrong time. He simply hadn't been willing to believe she'd been trapped here by accident. Regret made him as cold as the snow.

He wouldn't have been surprised if she'd pushed him away. Instead she held on to him fiercely, saying his name over and over as her hands pressed against his back, tunneled through his hair, clasped his upper arms.

His head turned. So did hers. A jolt of acute awareness shot through him when he realized his lips had found the softness of hers. For a breathless moment he waited to see if she'd pull away. She gasped with the contact. But she didn't withdraw. Instead she pressed against him, opening in an invitation that was as old as the heavens.

The kiss lengthened, deepened, seared. It should have melted the avalanche.

He hadn't planned the intimate contact. And he wasn't prepared for the impact. For the sheer, raw emotion that welled up inside him and crackled between them as he clasped her in his arms. He'd waited centuries to find her. In the endless moments when he'd dug frantically through the snow, he'd thought he'd lost her forever. The knowledge had left him cold and empty and shaken to the core.

Now he had a second chance, and he was still shaking. He'd never been so needy. So greedy. So hungry. His lips moved over hers with an urgency that took his breath away. Or perhaps it was the knowledge that she was responding with the same frantic exigency to be close, to give, to receive.

Lips, tongue, teeth. Moving, pressing, seeking. She sighed his name again, like a warm caress against his mouth. He was sure he'd never felt anything so erotic.

But in the next moment, she started shivering violently. Still, she held him tightly for another few seconds.

"Cassie...needs...warm."

She nodded, trying to keep her teeth from clattering together.

They were both breathing hard as they stumbled to their feet. He snatched up the flashlight from where he'd set it, and they started back the way they'd come, both staggering.

Inside the tunnel, the temperature was a little warmer but not much. Once inside the station, Cassie's face was grave as he opened drawers and pulled out as many blankets as he could find, draping them over her shoulders and his.

"Chicken soup," he managed to say. "Warm."

He was rewarded with a nod of understanding as she grabbed two more of the packets from her carry sack. Setting the flashlight where they'd both get some illumination, he took them from her.

When she tried to protest, he gestured toward the bed. "Cassie needs warm!"

She sat down, making a nest among the covers like a small bird seeking refuge. When she glanced up at him, he felt his throat tighten. He wanted to kneel and take her in his arms, tumble her to her side and press her body against his again. Instead, he stood with his arms folded across his chest.

Satisfied that she was settled, he took the packets to the grooming alcove. It wasn't difficult to make the chicken soup.

As he worked, his thoughts churned. He couldn't fool himself any longer. When he'd seen Cassie buried under the snow, his raw emotions had come screaming to the surface. In the few hours they'd spent together, she'd become very important to him. Yet coping with that admission made him acutely uncomfortable.

He didn't want to feel anything for this woman. So he tried to fill his thoughts with logical speculation. When he'd first awakened, he'd half expected to find armed guards outside. The snow blocking the entrance to the installation had put a different perspective on the situation. It seemed he and Cassie Devereaux were on their own. From the way she was dressed and the contents of her carry pack—it appeared she'd been on some kind of outdoor expedition when she'd gotten caught in an avalanche. He wasn't going to forget the meaning of that word anytime soon.

The rock ledge protecting the tunnel entrance had saved her life. But had she been alone? And why wasn't anyone looking for her? Or were they?

He'd delayed returning as long as he could. Finally he brought the chicken soup out to her and sat beside her.

He could see her wariness, see the questions in her posture as she pretended to concentrate on the simple meal. Or perhaps she wanted to tell him he was a damn fool for insisting on going out. But she only looked at him silently.

"Thorn...sorry," he said, the admission costing him more than he'd anticipated.

She went very still, her face shadowed so that he couldn't see her eyes. Finally she nodded and said something that he hoped was a gracious acceptance of the apology. When she draped one of the spare blankets over his legs, elation filled his chest.

He wanted to tell her a great deal. He wanted to ask why she'd kissed him as if the two of them meant something to each other. But confessions and questions were both beyond the limited vocabulary he'd been painfully acquiring. So he settled for keeping her close to him, acutely aware of her even though a few inches of space separated their shoulders.

The warmth of the cup brought a stinging pain to his fingers. That was good, he knew. It meant the nerves were coming back to life.

Cassie glanced at him and then away. He wanted to know what she was feeling, instead he took another sip of soup. He recognized the need for intimacy was dangerous. But he was too cold and weary to exercise much control.

CASSIE SILENTLY DRANK her soup, glancing every so often at Thorn from the corner of her eye, trying to rationalize her extraordinary response to him. The longer she stayed with him, the less she knew her own mind, and the more frustrated she felt. He was a complicated man. Intelligent. Strong willed. Arrogant. Proud. Mistrustful. At first he'd scared her to death. Then he'd made her ache to understand him. No. That wasn't true. Both reactions had been there from the beginning. Only the balance had shifted.

One thing she was sure of now, he cared what happened to her—even if he preferred to hide his strong feelings. The look of anguish on his features when he'd brushed the snow from her face had made her heart turn over and her arms go around him. Then he'd kissed her, and she'd felt the two of them spinning out of control, seeking to get as close as a man and a woman could get to each other. Lord, had she ever felt that kind of intensity before?

She continued sipping at her soup because it was warm and it gave her something to do while her thoughts churned.

They kept coming back to a few fundamental questions. Who was this man who seemed so lost one moment and so sure of himself the next? Where was he from? What was he doing here?

She felt his frustration that they couldn't talk. Yet at the same time she sensed he was relieved that he didn't have to answer a slew of questions.

She was too weary to come up with any coherent conclusions about him. In fact, by the time she finished the last of the broth, she stifled a yawn. Since she'd only been outside in the snow for a little while, it was probably safe to sleep, she decided, if she piled on the blankets. As she started to gather up several blankets and move away, Thorn put his hand over hers. Not with his commanding grip. This time his touch was very gentle. But he held her with the intensity of his gaze.

"Cassie cold. Thorn cold," he said very slowly, then cleared his throat and added, "Thorn...Cassie sleep—warm.'' He ended with a gesture that included the two of them and the bed.

So, after everything that had happened between them, he was inviting her to sleep with him.

When she didn't respond, he gave her a wry little smile. ''Thorn sleep night,'' he added.

Probably, with his limited vocabulary, it was an assurance that he wasn't making an indecent proposal. She pretended to inspect her hands as she watched him lie down. There was no reason to trust his word for anything except that he could have left her in that snowbank—except that he'd kissed her as if she were the most important thing in his universe. And she'd kissed him back with the same yearning need. The admission frightened her on a very profound level.

There was a long, pregnant silence as he pulled two blankets over himself, rolled to his side and lifted the edge of the covers.

Reason warred with a whole constellation of emotions in Cassie's breast. It was freezing in here, and sharing body heat made sense, if that was all he was offering. If that was all she wanted.

He watched her face. Watched her silent debate.

''Sleep. Okay,'' he said.

She nodded, wishing things between them weren't so complicated. Making her decision with a sudden finality, she came down beside him, her back to his front. He pulled the covers over her. When his arm went around her shoulder, drawing her close, she tensed. But he did nothing more threatening.

She switched off the flashlight, and the room was plunged into total blackness. The heavy darkness made her feel as if a weight were pressing against her chest. Her fingers closed around the cold barrel of the flashlight, but she didn't turn it on. They had to save the battery. So she closed her eyes against the night and pressed her back against Thorn's front, comforted by the hard wall of his chest.

He murmured something low and reassuring.

A few moments later, she knew by the deep, regular sound of his breathing that he was asleep. Well, at least he'd given up the notion that she was going to stab him in the back, she thought with a little sigh.

She was suddenly acutely aware that she was lying in bed with a man. Preparing to go to sleep with him—a risk she'd rarely taken.

She tried to put a little distance between herself and Thorn, but his arm had slipped over her shoulder, and she didn't want to chance waking him. So she lay in the dark, willing herself to breathe evenly and relax as she tried to figure out what made this man different from the rest. He was a man in trouble. Lord, he could be anything from an escaped criminal to a political prisoner. None of the scenarios she could conjure up inspired trust. She'd always opted for staying safe. Staying uninvolved. Yet some deep instinct had led her to lie down with him when trust was completely out of character. She kept thinking about that until her brain was too fatigued to cling to consciousness.

ZEKE CHAMBERS STARED at the screen of his laptop. The results from his latest analysis swam in and out of focus. But that wasn't surprising. He'd been inside this tent for eight hours straight, trying to translate the newly found tablets. The thirst for discovery, two cups of strong coffee and a couple of granola bars had kept him going. Thank God Marie had been as anxious as he to keep their find secret. Without her cooperation, he'd be sharing this stuff with half the team.

He still wasn't sure what he was dealing with—a clever hoax or an archaeological treasure.

It had taken him several hours to input the symbols via a graphics-design package into the system. Then he'd run a pattern match against a newly compiled data base with more than twenty-thousand entries of all the dead and living languages that had ever been discovered.

The screen beeped as the program finished its final analysis. Zeke blinked as he took in the results. There were only two partial matches—one found in a cave in Corsica and the other in Alaska.

With a fresh burst of energy, he pulled up more details. The Alaskan find was in 1955; the Corsican one in 1935. Neither discovery had ever been corroborated with additional material, and research money had soon fizzled. They'd both been reduced to mere footnotes of unexplained occurrences. Too bad the data base hadn't been around back then.

Zeke turned back to his original text. He'd made some progress with a few words that bore a resemblance to Greek.

He was logging in his notes when he heard a familiar voice. "It's Marie."

She ducked inside, a tray in her hands. "You worked through supper. You must be famished."

Zeke felt a pang of hunger stab through him as he caught a whiff of spicy lamb stew. "You guessed right. Thanks."

Moving two reference volumes to the floor, he made room on the table for the tray.

"Have you discovered anything about our little find?" she asked.

"Take a look at this analysis." He angled the screen so she could see.

She leaned over his shoulder.

"Hmm. Very interesting."

He had trouble focusing on her words. Her perfume was sweet. Sickly sweet. His lungs burned with the smell. He tried to get up and out of the tent into the fresh air. But his arms and legs wouldn't move.

"I feel sick," Marie choked out.

Her head slumped onto his shoulder. Then her body toppled to the floor. He wanted to catch her. Instead he tumbled along with her to the ground.

Through blurry eyes, he saw a man in coveralls and a gas mask enter the tent. Zeke watched legs step over his body and hands reach for the tablets.

"No," Zeke tried to shout, but the word never reached his lips. In the next moment his mind lost the fight for consciousness.

IT SEEMED LIKE only moments later when Cassie's eyes snapped open. She knew immediately that she was dreaming. In her sleep, she had finally escaped from the underground prison. With a sense of wonder and freedom, she looked around. She was standing in bright sunlight under an impossibly cloudless violet sky, on a rocky hillside dotted with strangely shaggy trees. The setting was so different from the buried bunker that it took her breath away.

She knew several things immediately. She had been here before. And everything that had happened since she'd started pulling strings to get the Alaskan assignment had been propelling her to this place. Or had it started before that?

Fear shimmered through her. Fear that she would discover some truth better left buried in her subconscious. She tried to wrench herself out of the dream, before it was too late, but it held her fast like a magician's spell. She looked around with new wariness. The scene appeared peaceful, but she felt danger pulsing in the air.

"It's just a dream," she murmured. Yet it was impossible to bring back the feeling of calm. Somehow this experience had its own reality, and it was more than the sum of its parts.

Below her was a small grove of trees that might have been pines, but their foliage was blue-red. She couldn't see through the branches, but she knew she had to go there. It was her only option. Her heart started to pound. The cautious part of her wanted to run in the other direction. The yearning part of her longed to go to the man who was hidden behind the trees.

Thorn. He was there. Somehow she knew he was waiting for her in this place. Had been waiting for a long time.

On feet that barely touched the ground, she moved toward the grove. Looking down at her body, she realized she was wearing delicate leather sandals and a filmy white tunic that dipped low between her breasts and hardly covered her thighs.

Thorn's choice. He wanted to see her that way.

She stepped between the blue-red trees and into a quiet courtyard that shut out the world. It was decorated with clay pots that held fragrant herbs and bright flowers she didn't recognize. Thorn was standing beside a low couch. A couch in a garden? Before she had time to ponder that, Thorn captured her attention. He was almost as naked as the first time she'd seen him, except that a strip of white cloth circled his waist and hung down in front, covering his sex. Otherwise, she had a wonderful view of his magnificent body. Her heart began to beat faster as she took in his broad shoulders, his flat stomach, his muscular thighs—all at the peak of health and vitality.

When she saw that he was staring at her with the same appreciation, she flushed and somehow kept from crossing her arms in front of her breasts. He, on the other hand, seemed totally at ease.

She had the strange sense that she had seen him standing like this before. Waiting for her.

"You brought me here," she whispered.

He looked surprised. "Did I?"

"Yes," she answered with absolute conviction. Then as a new realization struck her, she drew in a little breath. "Are we speaking English?"

"I do not know," he said, a look of wonder suffusing his features as he came toward her. "Is that what you call your language?"

"Yes."

"I can understand you."

"We can talk to each other," she marveled. "Finally. How is that possible?"

"I do not know." He reached out and touched her arm, her hair, her mouth. She moved her lips against his knuckle.

There were so many questions, so many choices. She forced herself to pick one. "Tell me," she demanded fiercely. "About the place where we're both sleeping now." She stopped abruptly, brought up short by the strangeness of the conversation. You didn't have dreams where you discussed your sleeping body.

The question made his eyes narrow dangerously. "It is a secret installation. Illegal, I would guess."

She felt goose bumps bloom on her skin. "Illegal?"

"Can you tell me where it is located? What part of the world?"

"Alaska. Near Denali National Park."

"That doesn't mean anything to me." His gaze turned speculative. "What were you doing there?"

Cassie hesitated for a moment, then decided to play it perfectly straight. "I was investigating an anomalous energy source for the Federal Communications Commission."

"How did you get there?"

"Airplane."

"Define."

"Uh, a craft that flies through the air. You've never heard of them?"

He ignored the question. "How is it powered?"

"With something called an internal combustion engine. There are faster planes with jet engines. I don't have the technical education to tell you how either kind works."

"Were you alone?"

"No. I came out here with a guide who knows the area. I think he died in the avalanche."

Thorn nodded gravely.

She frowned as she realized that he'd taken control of the conversation, that he'd been asking all the questions. "How did *you* arrive?" she demanded and watched him make a silent decision.

"I do not know for certain. Lodar drugged me and stashed me in the delta capsule."

"Lodar?"

"The expedition leader."

"Put that in terms I can understand," she demanded.

He shook his head. "I cannot."

"Can't? Or won't?"

He shrugged.

"How long have you been here?"

"I will not know until I can see the night sky." His face suffused with anger. And a deep fear. He masked the latter quickly.

"Why did he leave you in the chamber?"

"We were having a political dispute."

"So he—?"

"Isolated me from my people."

Her eyes widened. "Isn't that rather an extreme response?"

He laughed mirthlessly. "You do not know Lodar."

"You took a position he didn't like? What was it?"

He sighed. "This conversation is getting dangerous."

"For whom?"

"For me. For both of us." His face was etched with doubt and sadness. She might have taken him in her arms. But she had become too unsure.

Instead she asked the question that had been lurking at the back of her mind like a wild animal trying to escape from a cage. "What happens if the solar panels aren't working tomorrow?"

She heard his breath catch in his throat. "If the power remains off and we cannot get through that wall of snow, we will die."

Chapter Five

"No!" Cassie's hands dug into his shoulders. He stood rigid, his blue eyes burning down into hers.

"We will find out in the morning if the power cells have regenerated," he said, making no attempt at predictions.

She looked at the trees, the flowers and herbs growing in terra-cotta pots. At the gentle glow of the violet sky. Thorn had created their meeting place. Made it as different as he could from the sterile chamber where they slept.

"Can't we stay here?"

"No. The dream has its own reality. But it is not a permanent refuge."

"I'm frightened," she whispered, a fine tremor going through her body.

"Of tomorrow?"

"Of what is happening now."

"You mean here? Within this fantasy?" He sounded perplexed.

She nodded fractionally, suddenly honing in on a basic principle her subconscious had been playing with since the beginning of her strange encounter with Thorn. The way to know this man was not to ask him questions he'd only stonewall. The way to know him was to dig deep for answers within her soul. As soon as she admitted the possibility, she felt a door open in her mind.

"You've been trying to hide from me all along. But I know who you are," she blurted.

"Oh?" His blue eyes bored into her like diamond drills.

"I mean—" She groped for the right words and found them where she least expected. "I've had dreams like this before." She looked around again at the peaceful setting. "I've been *here* before. In this little courtyard. I recognize this place."

"Impossible."

She shook her head. Now that she'd stopped fighting the truth, details were coming to her with surreal clarity. "For years I've dreamed of a man who attracts me—powerfully." The words were dragged out of her almost against her will. "Someone I trust because I can't see his face."

"You are not making sense. What kind of twisted logic is that?" he demanded, his features etched with strain, his eyes probing.

She felt her face heat. Her nerve failed, and she looked away.

He didn't allow her to retreat. With a hand under her chin, he brought her gaze back to his. "Look at me. Tell me exactly what you mean."

She swallowed hard, wanting to run and hide from him, from herself. From the truth. Yet she knew deep inside that if she didn't say what was in her heart, she would destroy herself. "I—I never remember very much when I wake up. But after I've been with him,

I feel as if something very moving has happened between us.''

He continued to stare at her, his expression a mixture of scorn and defenselessness.

Part of her longed to snatch back the secret. Part of her rejoiced that she had finally confided in someone. For years she'd kept her strange dreams to herself. She hadn't even told her sister—the one person who might have understood. In fact, she knew that over the past few months the experience had become much more intense—because Marissa was paired with Jed. Cassie had been overjoyed at her sister's happiness. But she'd been envious, too. So she'd found herself coming back more and more often to her shadowy companion—and letting herself feel things she'd never allow in real life.

''You are telling me you have bonded with a man you have never met?''

She nodded slightly.

''Why?''

''It was safe. And...and I know he needs me. I'm his only link with the outside world.'' She swallowed convulsively. Yet she knew she had to finish what she'd started. ''Now I think...he's you. That's why I've felt connected with you since the beginning. Even when we couldn't speak to each other.''

His face registered total shock. ''Impossible,'' he said again. Yet the look deep in his eyes told her he might be trembling on the edge of belief.

''In that chamber—that delta chamber—did you call out to anyone? For help.''

He made a strangled sound. ''I do not remember my dreams. If I had dreams.''

''You're having this one,'' she said with conviction. "We both are. You brought me here," she insisted. "Again."

"What did we do in these dreams of yours?" he demanded.

Her heart squeezed as she remembered the intimacy. "Mostly...we...were just together. Warm and close. The way we're sleeping now. Sometimes I think we kissed. But...we didn't do anything...compromising. It was safe."

"Safe," he repeated. "You like that word."

She shrugged. She'd taken tremendous risks in every area of her life—except relationships. But she wasn't going to explain that to him.

His gaze drilled into her, and she knew he was still trying to reject her story. "It sounds as if you are describing a liaison with a man who was half-dead."

"No," she protested.

"And so were you," he accused. "You have admitted you lived through your dreams. With a man who was a stranger."

"Not live!" she denied automatically, weighted down by the harsh tone of his voice. "I—I have my work. It's very challenging. I have a lot of responsibilities. And I have friends."

"What are you afraid of in your real life?" he persisted.

She swallowed around the lump that blocked her windpipe. She didn't want to say it. A force beyond her control compelled her to admit her failings. "Loving," she said brokenly.

"Loving."

"Love means domination. Control of one person by another. I've known that since I was a little girl."

"That is no definition of love."

"It *was* in my family," she retorted, determined to keep the rest to herself. She wasn't going to talk about her painful childhood. About the father who'd demanded total obedience, who'd run his family like a military unit. Who'd made her afraid to reveal the tender core of her being.

"Cassie—?"

"Is this place familiar to *you?*" she asked, switching the conversation away from her crippled emotional development.

"It is in my garden," he said reluctantly. "At home."

"See..." She let the sentence trail off as if he'd offered her proof.

A fierce look captured his features, a look of male dominance that terrified her. "So you are saying I brought a beautiful woman here again and again. But I did not make love to her," he grated. "Do you expect me to believe that?"

"You were different," she whispered. "Undemanding. You needed me to be there—with you. Because you'd been alone for so long."

"Is *that* the kind of relationship you want?" he challenged.

"Yes," she whispered.

His eyes told her he didn't believe it. All at once, there was no place to hide. From herself. From him.

"Let us discover the truth," he challenged as he took her by the forearms.

She tried to back away, but he held her tightly. There was a charged moment of anticipation when she knew he would take what he wanted, and she would freely give. Then his mouth descended and moved over hers, ruthlessly, insistently.

Raw power flowed between them. Power and an erotic current so strong that it made her quake.

Everything had changed. There was no longer safety in this place. Only the knowledge that he was quaking, too, kept panic from swallowing her alive. She knew he was captive to the same elemental force. And that she held as much of the power in this encounter as he.

With a little moan, her mouth opened. In response, his softened, and the kiss took on a wholly different meaning. He shifted his head, capturing her lips from one angle and then another, taking and giving at the same time with a finesse that made her head spin. Lord, he knew how to kiss a woman. Knew how to arouse with a potency she had never experienced before.

She took and gave in return, tasting him, feasting from him as her hands moved restlessly across the wide expanse of his back, glorying in the touch of his naked skin under her fingertips.

She felt the tension in his body. Felt his arousal as he lifted her intimately against him. When his hand slipped inside the low-cut front of her tunic and teased her nipple, she sighed her pleasure and arched into his caress.

The kiss broke, and they both gasped for air as they clung to each other for stability. She looked at him and almost drowned in the wonder that deepened his eyes. Tenderly, she touched his flushed cheek, his lips, his thick eyelashes.

He took her lips again in another searing kiss, a kiss that acknowledged the passion that had smoldered between them for so long. Only now the rules had changed. He was no longer content with mere companionship. And neither was she. The power of her response to him left her knees weak. When she sagged against him, he scooped her up in his arms and carried her to the couch.

"I want you naked. Flesh to flesh," he growled as he set her down.

"Yes."

He knelt to unbuckle the sandals from her feet, and she braced her hands against his shoulder to keep from swaying. He turned his face to her, his hot breath scorching her middle, his lips teasing the apex of her legs through the thin fabric of her tunic.

She dug her fingers into his hair, holding him close. When he stood again, her blood was flowing in her veins like a river of fire.

"*Dubina,*" he whispered in his own language. "Dear one."

"My darling," she answered in a breathy sigh.

He knew where to find the clasp that held her bodice closed. Swiftly he swept the garment from her shoulders, stripped it off. Need exploded in her center as his hot gaze drifted over her. He was the only man who could make her feel this way. The only man who could satisfy the needs she hid from the world.

Her hands went to his waist, tugging at the place where the strip of cloth was fastened. She pulled it away, and there were no barriers between them.

He gasped as she caressed him. Then he carried her down to the yielding softness of the couch.

He turned her to her side, his hands stroking over her body, starting with her legs, her stomach. His teeth worked an erotic path up her neck to her jaw, then down again to her breasts, kindling throbbing heat at the center of her desire.

"Please. I want you," she whimpered. "I've waited so long for this."

"So have I," he answered as she arched and twisted against his hands and mouth.

"Please. If you don't...I—"

CASSIE NEVER GOT a chance to finish the sentence. There was a rush of sound. A jarring flash of light. And she cried out again. But this time it was from shock and surprise at the rapid change of scene.

She was still in Thorn's arms. That was the only constant in a wildly shifting universe. But the courtyard and the couch had vanished. Now they were lying on the blankets she'd spread on the stone floor of the installation. And they were wearing the clothes they had on when they went to sleep. Except that her jacket was off, and the front of her shirt was pulled up around her neck.

She blinked in the harsh lights from above. The generators were working again. The sun had come up, and the solar collectors had absorbed enough power to reactivate the installation.

Her fingers still dug into Thorn's shoulder. Caught in the throes of passion, he tried to pull her body more tightly against his. She wrenched out of his grasp and rolled away from him.

"Cassie."

The jarring end to the dream sent her emotions reeling. "No! It's not real. It never was," she said brokenly.

His body went rigid. His hands clenched at his sides. She watched him sucking in great gasps of air as he struggled to get control of his aroused body.

She pulled down her shirt and closed her eyes, trying to cope with the warring emotions hammering at her heart—and the sexual need shimmering through her. She was on fire and at the same time reduced to ashes.

She lay listening to the harsh sound of her own breathing—and his—and thinking about the trap she'd fallen into. She'd told him intimate, personal things she'd never dared to confide to anyone else. They bombarded her now, and she struggled to hold back tears. What had seemed so right—so possible—in the warm cozy dream was now beyond her reach.

Yet she felt totally open, totally vulnerable to him.... Unless everything that had just happened was simply her fantasy.

She sat up and pressed her fingers against her lips, intent on moving away to some private place where she could think. Where she could calm down and figure out what to do. As she started to scramble to her feet, Thorn grabbed her hand.

She wouldn't look at him.

"Do not...run...from me."

Her head jerked toward him.

"Do not hide," he added.

He'd spoken haltingly, but still with vastly more assurance than she'd ever heard in this room. She didn't have to ask him how he'd suddenly gotten so proficient in English. She knew. It was from the dream. While they'd been together in that other place, speaking, the language barriers had come down. And as they'd talked to each other, he'd picked up a wealth of English vocabulary and syntax.

Cassie sighed. Any hope she'd entertained that the erotic encounter had simply been her fantasy evaporated. He'd been there with her, all right. And his computer-sharp brain would remember every word she'd said.

He sat up and realized his shirt was half-off. Flushing, he tugged it down.

That was her only consolation. Now that the interlude was over, he was as embarrassed as she by what had happened.

The silence between them stretched. He looked toward the ceiling and cleared his throat. "The sun...the solar panels must be..." He paused.

"Operational," she supplied.

"We have to talk about what happened," he said, shattering her false sense of security.

"I can't."

He took her hand again, his flesh warm and firm as he clasped her fingers. She didn't want to feel anything. But she couldn't suppress the sexual jolt that transmitted itself from his hand to hers.

"It was only a dream." She knew her eyes revealed how much she wanted him to accept her version of the truth.

"You believe that?"

"It's my best option."

He sighed. "You are safe from personal discussions for now. I must check..." There was another pause while he searched his vocabulary. "...the communications."

"That's one of the first things I tried. It's how I got shocked," she retorted, determined to keep the conversation neutral.

His eyebrow lifted. "You know how to operate the...analyzers?"

"We call them computers," she said wearily.

"All right, computers. Did Lodar teach you how to use them?"

She made a gesture of exasperation. "I haven't met Lodar. I thought I might be able to figure out the equipment—given enough time."

"I doubt that."

"You doubt what? My intentions or my intellect?"

Ignoring the jibe, he crossed to the terminal where she'd gotten into trouble.

"Watch out," she warned, unable to stop herself from rushing to his side in case something happened.

"I do not have many choices." He looked at the desktop. Then he quickly lowered his hand, pressing the palm flat against the cold surface.

Cassie held her breath. When there was no crackle of electricity, she let out the breath she was holding.

He began speaking in a clipped voice—in his own language. And she acknowledged she'd have had zero chance of running the machine. However, with Thorn in command, the screen came to life. No, she corrected herself. Screens. In addition to the one at the terminal, there were six others at various locations around the room. Two of them were four-feet square. The others were smaller. All of them had blended into the walls so completely that she hadn't known they were there. Now they buzzed and crackled with a pattern of shimmering black dots like a television when the cable signal is cut off.

Cassie shivered. What was this place?

Thorn made an adjustment, and the crackling faded into the background. He kept speaking to the machine.

"I cannot raise the base," he finally said. "Or—"

He stopped abruptly. "Not even an automatic homing signal. Everything is gone. Vanished."

She could see he was struggling with emotions she could only guess.

"Who are you trying to contact? Maybe the equipment here is broken."

"We will see," he grated. Grim faced, he sat down in front of the console and began to speak again.

Cassie took the other chair.

One of the big screens went from fuzzy static to a black-and-white picture. Of all things, it showed an old "I Love Lucy" rerun. The famous episode where Lucy is in labor and Desi rushes to the hospital straight from his nightclub—dressed in a witch-doctor costume.

Thorn stared at the picture assessingly. "You have satellite broadcasts," he mused. "Transmission of pictures and sound."

"Of course."

"Black-and-white only?"

"It's an old program. We've had color for forty years." Cassie swallowed as she grappled with the unreality of the conversation. "Thorn, why do you not know any of that? Where are you from, really?" she asked with sudden determination.

"You probably would not believe me."

"Let me decide that."

"Just think of me as part of an experiment—a man who has been isolated from the world for many years. My survival depends on learning as much as I can about present conditions."

"Your survival," she echoed, a shiver going over her flesh.

"Yes. Help me with what I need to know." He

gestured toward the TV episode—with Lucy's swollen abdomen and Desi's mask and drum. "Are fertility rites broadcast during important festivals?"

Cassie laughed, dissipating some of the tension. "No. You're watching what's called a situation comedy." She went on to explain the episode.

Thorn nodded, and she wondered how much he'd understood given the seriousness with which he posed outrageous questions.

He issued more commands to the computer. A variety of pictures flashed onto the wall screens. A close-up of a flower opening its petals. "Donahue." *The Big Chill.* A laundry-detergent commercial.

His attention flicked from one to the other. Every few seconds he stopped to freeze a frame and query her.

Cassie stood rigid beside him. She felt as disoriented as if she were back in the dream. The implications of Thorn's reactions to the television broadcasts and his questions were so staggering that she couldn't cope with them. Her mind refused to function with its normal efficiency. All she could do was deal with tiny bits of information one at a time. "We clean most clothes in water at home. Some go to what's called a dry-cleaning shop where they're processed with chemicals.... A microwave doesn't utilize a heat source. It cooks food quickly by bombarding it with high-frequency radio waves. Or maybe it's low frequency.... Popcorn is the exploded kernel of a grain called corn. We eat it as a snack."

She blushed when she realized a porno flick had caught his attention.

"They broadcast that?" he asked, incredulous.

She swallowed hard. "Some people like to watch."

Thorn issued more commands, focusing on one screen and then another. ''Sesame Street'' drew another question.

''That's a show for children,'' Cassie explained. ''Big Bird's a fantasy animal whose behavior is child-like—so the kids can identify with him. There's an actor inside the costume.''

After flipping to a couple of commercials, he found CNN. In rapid succession he watched relief efforts for earthquake victims, a woman who'd stabbed her abusive husband, a riot at a soccer stadium where half a dozen fans were trampled to death, and the tearful wife of a German tourist murdered in Florida.

''So much violence,'' Thorn whispered.

''News programs focus on it,'' Cassie told him, knowing the explanation was inadequate.

The camera cut away from the anchorman to a globe spinning against a blue background. Thorn slowed the speed, then stopped the frame on the Mediterranean and eastern Europe. ''Where are we now?''

''On the other side of the world.''

He played the saved picture, spinning the sphere to get an overview. Then he advanced the picture until the appropriate land masses filled the screen.

She pointed to Alaska. ''We're about four hundred miles inland.''

''Miles. I do not know the unit of measurement.''

Cassie searched her memory for a math fact. ''A mile is 5,280 feet. A foot is twelve inches, about like this.'' She held her hands apart.

He studied the map. ''We are very far north. Is it the warm time of year in this region?''

''Yes. Summer.''

''The days are abnormally long?''

She nodded.

"And in winter, they are short."

"Yes."

His features were thoughtful. "Then the solar collectors must have a long-term storage capacity. That is probably lucky." He turned away from the screens and issued more instructions to the computers. A diagram in shades of green appeared on the glassy monitor mounted in the back of the desk. He moved his hand on the horizontal surface, and various parts of the picture changed colors.

"What are you doing?" Cassie asked.

"Surveying this station. It is bigger than I expected. There is a sleep chamber and a place to prepare nourishment."

Working rapidly, he used his hand to change the colors on the monitor. Each shift was now accompanied by activity around the station. Purple. She heard motors turn behind closed doors. White. A fan went on and clicked off again. Yellow. Lights flickered and came on more brightly. Blue. Water ran in the sink.

Several areas changed to orange on the screen. "Supply depots," he explained. "I want to see the inventory."

Thorn was focused intently on what looked like a list of items when the lights in the room dimmed.

"What?" he muttered, his hand moving rapidly over the surface of the desk as he spoke to the computer. "It is not responding. The controls are frozen."

"You didn't do that?" Cassie asked.

Thorn's answer was interrupted by a loud whistling sound that set her teeth on edge. Feeling as if her eardrums would burst, she clasped her hands over her ears.

"Please. Make it stop," she gasped, knowing Thorn couldn't hear above the high-pitched whistle.

He was out of his seat, his body rigid, his face contorted as he stared at the large television screen directly opposite them.

Chapter Six

The whistling faded away. Thorn gripped the edge of the work surface, unable to tear his gaze from the viewer. He stared into what appeared to be a plushly appointed office with a work surface of polished onyx, a chair of soft leather and a high-speed miniaturized analyzer for fieldwork. But the appointments were of minimal interest. What riveted his attention was the man seated behind the desk.

He had copper-colored skin, handsome features and a look of arrogance in his eyes meant to set him above ordinary mortals.

"Lodar," Thorn gasped, still fighting to understand what was happening. Against all odds, was his enemy really here?

Thorn might have rushed across the room toward the newly revealed room, except that Cassie was holding his arm in a death grip.

"That's him? The man who put you here?" she asked in a hoarse voice.

Thorn nodded.

"What's happening?" she begged. "I thought—"

He cut her off with a curt "I do not know." Then he lifted his head toward the man behind the desk.

"What do you want?" he challenged, speaking in their mutual language.

Lodar didn't answer. Instead he sat with the same arrogant stare and his hands clasped easily on the black stone in front of him.

Thorn's own fists were clenched. His pulse pounded in his ears. "Say something, you klat worm!" he shouted.

"Good morning, Thorn. Or is it evening in your little corner of the world? I trust you slept well. If you are viewing this recording, then you've made it out of the delta cylinder. And you have the satisfaction of knowing that your subversive theory was correct. The primitives here have advanced considerably in technology since we impressed them with our 'powers.' For all the good that's going to do you." Lodar laughed, a cruel, grating sound.

"Tell me what he's saying," Cassie whispered urgently.

"It is a three-dimensional recording. Let me listen!" Thorn muttered in English, before turning his full attention to the image of the man who had sent him into exile.

A recorded message. Of course. The illusion had been so perfect—so startlingly unexpected—that it had fooled him.

"Are the natives outside around their camp fire? Or are they with you—confounded by this show of awesome power? But that's your worry, not mine. You can decide what you wish to tell them. It won't matter to me anymore. The rest of us will be long gone by the time you see this message. Only the senior officers know that we received a recall order several cycles ago. That is why I acted so quickly to neutralize the threat you represent. I did not want you coming back to the Central Council, spouting your outrageous nonsense about respecting conquered peoples. If they want to worship us like gods, that's their business. Personally, I think they have learned quite a bit from the association with us. Certainly they have improved their gene pool.'' He laughed again.

Cassie tried to ask a question. Thorn waved her to silence.

''I will tell you what has been done,'' Lodar continued. ''I would have liked to have killed you. Unfortunately, when it came to murder, I couldn't override the moral training that was drummed into us from birth. However, I think I have worked around the prohibition rather nicely. I've had an underground facility adapted just for you, with a homing device that can only be detected by sophisticated instruments. It's quite far from our base camp. In an uninhabited area. And very well hidden, I might add. So it will take considerable technological advancement on the part of the natives to find it. Probably several thousand years.''

Thorn nodded. That had been his guess. He'd find out soon enough exactly how long.

''I am profoundly sorry you won't have a chance to say goodbye to your children. I've told Reah and Januk that you met with an unfortunate accident while on a fact-finding mission for me. The girl is very sad. The boy is trying to be stoic.''

Thorn's heart gave a lurch inside his chest. Since he had awakened, he had deliberately steered his mind away from the subject of his daughter and son—knowing he couldn't stand the pain of thinking about them. Now Lodar was ripping open a raw wound.

"But I think there's an excellent chance they can be adopted into a good family back home. A responsible husband and wife who will see they get a traditional education that will foster the correct values."

Thorn couldn't stifle a sound that was half gasp, half curse. Correct values! He hated the ideology that had bred a worm like Lodar.

"What?" Cassie whispered.

"My children," he answered brokenly before doggedly forcing his attention back to the recorded image. He didn't want to listen to any more of Lodar's gloating. But he had to pay attention.

The recorded image continued to speak. "I should remind you of one last important point. Remember those immunizations we all had to take? I checked the life-support logs. You were almost due for a booster. So I would suggest you get back to the base camp as soon as possible and give yourself an injection. I have left you some serum in a protected storage compartment—along with some other things you're doubtless going to need. Let's hope for your sake that the cache survived the centuries. And that you have adequate transportation."

Thorn stood rigid, staring at Lodar, hatred and anguish seething in his breast. He would never get home. And his survival depended on what might be an impossible journey. But his own predicament wasn't as important as the suffering of his children. Since Sanda's death, he had made sure Reah and Januk knew they were safe and loved. Lodar had yanked him away from the two people in all the universe who needed him most.

A cry welled in Thorn's throat. "No! No," he screamed. He wanted to spring at Lodar and wrap his hands around the man's fleshy neck. He wanted to squeeze the life out of him. But Lodar was as far beyond reach as Reah and Januk.

As he stared at the recording, flames sprang up around the man behind the work surface, consuming his image and the cozy little office where he sat. Thorn was so deep in shock that it took several seconds for him to realize that the conflagration wasn't part of the show.

It was real.

The temperature rose. The control room filled rapidly with smoke. Beside him, Cassie gasped. Then she started to cough and doubled over.

Thorn's eyes stung, and his chest heaved. Grabbing Cassie's hand, he pulled her to the floor. "Stay down."

She crouched, her face contorted as she gasped and stared at the flames licking at the wall beside the screen.

"There should be a...a—" He couldn't find the word in her language. Abandoning the explanation, he crawled to the first analyzer table and felt along the bottom surface.

Nothing.

The smoke stung his eyes, burned his lungs. Trying to hold his breath, he debated whether to grab Cassie and pull her to the entrance tunnel. But then what? They might escape the fire, but they couldn't dig themselves through the wall of snow.

As his mind scrambled to make life-and-death decisions, his fingers searched under the next worktable. Finally they closed around a cold metal object. In the next moment, he was coughing violently.

The smoke was so thick he could hardly see to aim

the douser. As he crawled toward the screen, Cassie grabbed his ankle.

"No."

Thorn wrenched out of her grasp and stood. Even a few feet from the floor, the choking fumes were like acid in his lungs. Working by touch alone, he depressed the controls and aimed the spout. A stream of chemical spray shot from the device, coalescing into droplets as it hit the flames. In a matter of seconds, they sputtered, went out. But he continued to play the stream over the ruined mess.

Finally he was satisfied that the fire was out. But the oxygen level in the room was still dangerously low. Thorn sank to a sitting position, trying to take shallow breaths, trying to fight the dizziness that threatened to swallow him up.

It would be so easy to simply lie on the floor and go to sleep. After the message from Lodar, it didn't matter much whether he lived or died. But if he didn't make it, neither would Cassie.

He turned his head and tried to locate her. His vision was too blurred from the fumes. Cursing, he got to his knees. Somehow he made it back to the analyzer. Somehow he pushed himself high enough to reach the work surface. Leaning over the console, he began to issue terse instructions. So distorted was his voice that the machine didn't respond. His head spinning, he made an effort to speak slowly and distinctly.

Precious seconds ticked by. He cleared his throat and tried again. When hidden fans began to whir, he knew he'd succeeded in communicating his orders. As the smoke started to clear, he anxiously scanned the room. His heart leapt when he spotted the heel of Cassie's boot several feet in front of the desk. But the elation was short-lived. She lay unmoving with her hands above her head—still as death.

Calling her name brought a spasm of coughing that made his chest burn and tears slide down his cheeks. She didn't stir.

"Cassie!"

He still didn't have the strength to walk. The best he could do was move toward her on hands and knees, doggedly putting one in front of the other.

It was like slogging through deep sand across an endless desert. Finally he reached her side and paused to catch his breath. The air was better. Pressing his hand gently against her chest, he gave thanks for the shallow rise and fall.

Later he didn't remember how he got Cassie across the room. Certainly he couldn't have carried her. But somehow he maneuvered the two of them to one of the doors that had not yet been opened.

Hoping he remembered the facility's schematic correctly, he palmed the release mechanism and waited for the barrier to slide into the wall. His sense of time was so distorted that it seemed to take several centuries.

After dragging Cassie across the threshold, he worked the interior latch mechanism, sealing off the remaining smoke in the control room. The lights had come on automatically as they entered. For long seconds, all he could do was sit with his back against the door, drawing in blessed oxygen as he looked around. They were in a small but comfortable sleeping chamber with a thick carpet and gently curving walls.

His chest didn't feel too bad. But when he swallowed, he discovered his throat was raw. For several moments he was too weary to move. As he sat with his head flung back, his mind served up questions. Had Lodar rigged that little surprise? Or was the station falling apart around their ears?

He'd have to do a full diagnostic. Later.

There was no question of getting Cassie onto the bed. So he simply turned her over on the carpet. Her eyes were closed and soot streaked her pale skin.

He wished he could get her to a healing station so he could find out what the smoke had done to her lungs. That was hardly an option. Wetting his finger in his mouth, he held it under her nose. Her breath was slow and steady. As he peered anxiously into her face, he saw some of the color was returning.

He closed his eyes as he flattened his palm against her chest, feeling the reassuring beat of her heart. He was half-dead. Still, it was impossible not to think about the way her breasts had felt in his hands. About the way they'd looked in the dream. Alabaster, with beautiful coral tips. He'd never seen such a color combination. And he hadn't been prepared for the raw pain he'd felt when she'd awakened and pushed him away. He had lost so much. But he had no right to bind her to him simply because he needed her.

She stirred slightly.

"Cassie? Just sleep, *dubina.*"

Incredibly, she spoke his name. "Thorn."

He sighed out a shuddering breath and gently stroked his fingertips across her cheek. Unconscious, she had called to him.

At first he hadn't believed what she had told him in the dream, that he'd brought her to his garden before. But how else could he account for the warm, familiar feeling of closeness that had wrapped itself around them? Despite his vow only moments ago, temptation was like a drug, pulling him toward her. All he had to do was lie down beside her and sleep, and they'd be back in the dream once again. Together. In a place where the problems of the world didn't exist. And she would come to him with the familiar loving warmth he craved.

They would both seem well and healthy. But he wouldn't know whether she was really unharmed, and he couldn't take that risk.

Instead he went to the small analyzer in the corner and temporarily boosted the oxygen level in the room. Then he flopped down beside Cassie for several more minutes, covering her hand with his, watching her sleep. The increased oxygen helped. Finally, he felt well enough to get up.

Cautiously he crossed to the door and palmed the control panel, opening the barrier a crack. The fans he'd turned on had done their work, and only a trace of smoke remained in the control room.

Good. Because he had work to do.

First he opened the healing cabinet and got out three cutaneous patches—a bright blue one and a small green one for him and a larger green one for Cassie.

His footsteps were light. But when he reentered the room, she stirred.

As he knelt, her lids fluttered. Slowly, her eyes opened and focused on him, and the terrible knot of tension in his chest loosened a little.

"How are you?" he whispered.

She seemed to consider the question carefully. He watched her take a cautious breath and let it out slowly.

"I passed out," she finally whispered.

He nodded.

She tried to sit up. He kept a gentle hand on her shoulder. "Lie still. You need to rest."

Cassie turned her head and looked at the unfamiliar surroundings. "Is this another dream?" she whispered, her voice slightly hoarse.

"No. We are safe. In a sleeping chamber."

"The fire..." Her eyes widened and she looked with alarm at the door.

"I put the flames out."

Several seconds elapsed before she spoke again. "You dragged me out of there."

"Yes."

Her eyes were bright and focused on him with a new understanding. "Thank you."

He wasn't prepared for the way her gaze stripped away his defenses. "Does it hurt to breathe?"

"No." Her voice was still gritty.

"Your throat?"

She swallowed, winced and nodded.

"You need to sleep and get your strength back. Do you want water?"

She nodded.

He brought a cup, lifted her head and helped her drink. Then he eased her back to a supine position.

"I am going to give you some medicine—something that is absorbed through the skin. When you wake up, you will feel much better."

He stripped the backing from the larger green patch and pressed it to her neck.

"Wait." She tried to pull his hand away. He held the patch in place until her lids fluttered. Then he took it off again.

"Sleep, *dubina.*"

In minutes she sank into a deep, healing slumber.

First he gave himself a smaller dose of the same healing medication. Then with a grimace, he pressed the blue patch to the other side of his neck and waited until the drug hit his system. It was a powerful stimulant, and he probably shouldn't be using it in combination with the other medication. But he had a great deal of work to do. He felt an immediate jolt. His senses sharpened, and his emotions surged out of control. For a second, his logical mind was swamped by the overload. If Lodar had been in the room, he would have grabbed the man's neck and squeezed. He'd never felt that kind of anger. It was so alarming, he dug his fingers into the carpet to steady himself. Eyes closed, he called on the techniques he'd learned in training. With deep breathing he brought himself under control.

Lifting Cassie's hand, he pressed her knuckles against his lips. Then he covered her with a light blanket and slipped a pillow under her head.

In the grooming alcove, he filled a cup with water for himself. It made his throat feel a little better. The smell of smoke clung to his clothing and body, and he looked longingly at the molecular cleaner. But he wasn't going to use up his precious time merely getting comfortable.

Pausing in the entryway to the control room, he surveyed the scene of the fire. The damage was surprisingly minor, considering the amount of smoke. Only the screen Lodar had used was totally ruined. The black streaks fanning out along the walls on either side were worse than they looked. The stone walls hadn't burned, and none of the other equipment appeared to be damaged. Even the smell of soot had been mostly filtered from the air.

After taking a seat at the console, he began to query the analyzer. The first news was good, he decided with an ironic snort. The fire was a deliberate accident arranged by Lodar and not a result of equipment failure. At least he knew the station wasn't disintegrating.

The problem with the solar collectors was also not as bad as he feared. They appeared to have been damaged by the avalanche that had trapped Cassie. The third panel was automatically taking over the work load of the other two.

Next he inventoried the supply rooms and cabinets, making note of particularly useful items. Yet all the time he knew in his heart he was stalling. He didn't want to confirm the worst, but he had to know.

The station was equipped with an outdoor camera that periodically photographed the night sky from a variety of angles. Thorn brought up the pictures, made a composite and studied the result. He could tell nothing from the casual inspection. But the analyzer would give him the information he sought. For a moment he hesitated. Then he requested a comparison of the present star chart with the first one the station had made.

"How many years separated the two views?" he asked.

The machine made rapid calculations and answered, "Two thousand, eight hundred and fifty-five years."

Thorn felt his throat close. For several seconds it was difficult drawing a full breath, as if the weight of the mountain above him were pressing down on his body, crushing him to oblivion. Carefully he went through the process again, checking the current sky with the view when Lodar had sealed him his fate.

When he asked the question again, he got the same answer. Two thousand, eight hundred and fifty-five years.

For long moments he sat rigid in the chair, staring at the screen, trying to make his mind absorb the information. He'd known he was far from home. He hadn't dared contemplate the length of his exile. Now—

A noise made him turn.

Cassie was standing by the door, inspecting the damage to the room. When she saw he was watching her, she gave him a little smile and gestured toward the only place where the fire damage was visible. "I think we lucked out."

"Lucked out. As in acquired good fortune?"

She nodded and he didn't argue the point.

"How do you feel?" he asked.

"Better than you, I think," she said in a quiet voice as she gave his face the same inspection she'd given the room. "Have you been busy here all the time I was sleeping?"

He nodded, then stretched, trying to work the kinks out of his muscles.

She came closer and peered at the ruined screen. "Did you figure out what started the fire?"

He had made a decision as he'd watched her lying unconscious on the rug. He was never going to be anything but honest with her again, no matter what it cost him. "Lodar coded a malfunction into his tape."

"I couldn't understand what he was saying," Cassie whispered.

Thorn felt his face harden. "He was gloating."

Cassie touched his shoulder, then she knelt so that her face was almost at his eye level. "You said he was talking about your children. And...and you looked so anguished. Did he do something to them?" she asked urgently.

"You mean kill them?" Thorn choked out. "No." He closed his eyes and fought to keep from being swallowed alive by pain so intense it felt as if his insides were torn and bleeding. After several seconds he was able to continue. "He pointed out that I will never see them again."

"You love them very much." It wasn't a question. Cassie's voice carried absolute conviction.

He didn't trust himself to speak. His soul was still too flayed. So he nodded tightly and didn't bother to correct her verb tense. Not love. Loved. Referring to the past. He'd thought he was scientifically sophisticated. He was still having trouble grappling with the concept of traveling so far while standing in one spot. Mercifully, Cassie seemed to sense that he didn't want to answer any more questions. She laid her head on his knees and wrapped her arms around his waist. He wanted to ask what she was feeling. But he'd vowed to demand nothing from her. The silence between them stretched. Finally he cast around for something to say. "Your clothes are smoky. You need to get cleaned up."

"Umm."

He helped her to her feet. When she swayed, he steadied her with his hands under her elbows. She leaned back against him and sucked in a long breath.

"Okay?"

"I'm dizzy, but it's going away."

"The medicine sometimes does that. It should not last too long."

"What did you give me?"

"A drug that induces sleep while it heals the body."

"You were in the fire, too—crawling around while I was unconscious. You don't need any healing?"

"I took some of the drug, as well. But I could not sleep. I had too much work to do."

He led her back to the sleeping chamber and opened one of the storage compartments. As he shifted through the contents, he could see that they hadn't been prepared specifically with him in mind. Lodar had simply shoved in modular units when he'd put the facility together. The logical conclusion was that he hadn't had much time to plan the kidnapping—for all the good that did Thorn.

Cassie pulled a lock of hair to her nose. "It's not just my clothes that smell awful."

"You can clean yourself in the grooming alcove." He pointed to the door he'd left open.

"Is there something resembling a shower?"

"Shower? You clean your bodies in the rain?"

She gave a spontaneous little laugh that did a lot to convince him she was recovering. Then her expression changed abruptly to pain.

He gripped her arm. "Are you sick?"

This time her laugh was harsh. "No. Assaulted by a bad memory. I played out in the rain and mud once. I was remembering what happened when my father came home and found I'd gotten my clothes muddy."

"He used laundry detergent to make them whiter than white?" he quoted a phrase from television.

"I wish." She gave him a sad smile. "He threw them in the garbage and whipped me with a strap."

Thorn stared at her. "Your father...whipped you. Like a...a farmer would whip his oxen?"

Her cheeks colored. "He believed in discipline."

"I do not understand. You discipline with love, not with physical punishment."

"When you love your children," she retorted.

"Is whipping offspring usual in your society?"

"That's hard to say. Most people who beat their kids don't do it in public."

He couldn't keep the horror out of his voice. "What kind of world do you come from?"

"One with...problems."

"Tell me—"

Her face darkened. "I'm not in any shape to defend society."

"I am sorry. I have no right to interrogate you."

She sighed wearily. "I'll feel better when I'm cleaned up."

"I understand. So will I."

"You could go first," she offered.

"After you."

She nodded fractionally. "So tell me what to do. In our bathrooms, we have a little stall where you stand under a spray of water and clean your body. You lather soap on your skin and use shampoo on your hair. Do you have those?"

"Not precisely."

He took her into the grooming alcove and pressed on the wall. A niche opened. "When you step inside, there is a mist of cleansing molecules."

She looked somewhat doubtful. "I...I'll take your word for it."

"Watch." He stuck his arm inside. The air within the chamber glowed a soft pink. When she looked closely, she saw tiny points of light dance over Thorn's hand and up his sleeve. "You will find it refreshing."

"All right."

"I do not like leaving you alone so soon after you have wakened from the healing drug. But I respect your nudity taboo."

"It's not a taboo."

"What is it?"

"Uh—"

"I will give you privacy. But I will be outside if you need me."

Cassie clutched the fresh clothing Thorn had given her as she watched him turn resolutely away from the bathroom door. Almost at once, he vanished from her line of vision. When he didn't reappear, she knew he must be guarding the entrance like a sentry. She almost shouted for him to go away and lie down, but she knew it wouldn't do any good. Sighing, she shoved the clothes he'd given her onto a little shelf. The effort left her breathless and light-headed. With a curse, she flattened a steadying hand against the wall and sucked in several lungfuls of air.

"Are you all right?" Thorn called.

"Yes. You don't need to stand right outside."

"I will stay."

Cassie nodded silently. One thing she'd learned, there was no use arguing with Thorn when he had made up his mind about something. Leaning against the edge of the sink, she struggled to breathe normally as she tried to cope with her swirling emotions as well as her weakened condition.

Lord, in the past twenty-four hours she felt as if she'd been swept away by a cyclone. Yet there was always one overwhelming constant at the center. Thorn.

Her eyes squeezed shut as her mind flashed back over every moment that had passed between them. Including the dream. When she'd awakened, she'd been frightened of the intimacy that had built between them. Not just the physical closeness. The sense of openness—of caring. She'd never dared let herself feel that way about anyone except her sister. And with Marissa it was different because it lacked the sexual component of a man and a woman powerfully attracted to each other.

Cassie tugged her shirt over her head and let it drop from her hand. On a deep, unconscious level, she'd longed for someone who could love her and accept her love in return. Yet even in her dreams, she'd been cautious. She'd opened up because she could pretend she was only playing with a fantasy. It had been a shock to discover that Thorn was as genuine as the avalanche that had trapped her here. The sudden realization had made her feel dangerously vulnerable. Uncertain. Terrified.

She glanced quickly toward the door, then away, half-afraid that he could read her thoughts. When he didn't come charging into the room, she breathed out a little sigh. Still, she knew he was out there. Because he was worried about her. Because he wanted to protect her.

It was hard to believe in those sentiments. Yet she would do the same thing if the situation were reversed.

"Do you need my help?" Thorn called out.

Cassie gulped, realizing that he was listening intently to her every move. But she hadn't been moving; she'd been standing and musing. "I'll be finished in a minute."

"How do you feel?"

"Better," she answered, realizing it was true. The medicine had improved her physical condition immeasurably. But her emotions were still in turmoil.

After a quick glance toward the place where she knew Thorn was standing, she unhooked her bra and skinned off her panties.

Wishing the "shower" stall had a door, she stepped inside. Immediately, the air changed. Pinpoints of light clustered over her skin, and she felt a strange tingling take possession of her body. Unprepared for the sensation, she couldn't hold back a startled gasp.

A millisecond later, Thorn charged into the room, his face tense with alarm. As he crossed to her, she automatically shrank back against the wall and raised one arm in front of her breasts. His hands were already on her shoulders.

"Cassie, are you hurt?"

"I—I wasn't expecting..." She gulped and started again. "The molecules s-startled me," she stammered.

The color of his cheeks deepened and he swore under his breath. "I am sorry. I was worried."

She gave him a tiny nod. "I know."

They stood looking into each other's eyes, sharing a wealth of emotions. He loosened his hold. But instead of letting go, his hands slid down her arms. The combination of his fingers touching her and the tingling sensation of the molecules made her shiver. She knew from the way the blue of his eyes deepened that he felt it, too.

"I should get out of here and give you your privacy," he said in a rough voice.

But he didn't.

Chapter Seven

Perhaps she held him with her heated gaze, because he didn't move. Time seemed to stand still. And the world shifted below her.

"Thorn." As if they had a will of their own, her arms slid around his neck. She had never felt more defenseless. Or more bold.

Trembling, she lowered her head to his shoulder.

A deep sigh shuddered out of him. Gently his fingers sifted through her hair, down her back, and across her hips. Everywhere he touched, the chamber's molecules shimmered on her skin, intensifying the tactile sensations, making her want to know what it would feel like with her fingers against *his* skin. Blindly, her hands found the hem of his shirt and tugged it up as she slid her fingers over his ribs.

"Cassie, do not."

Her heart wrenched, then began to pound frantically in her chest. The dream they'd shared could be reality. If she had enough courage. "Do you want me to stop?"

He made a low sound that might have been part curse, part prayer. Stepping away, he pulled the shirt over his head and tossed it with her clothes on the floor. Then his hands went to the waistband of his pants. In one smooth motion, he skimmed them over his hips and down his legs.

She stood without moving, her eyes taking in his superb male body, hard muscles, copper skin. It was as if a Greek god had come to life in this little room—and come to claim her as his own.

The first time she'd seen him like this—it seemed centuries ago—she'd been quaking inside. And she was still quaking. But not for the same reasons. Back then the two of them had been wary strangers. Now—

Now he was magnificently aroused. Yet he didn't cross the space between them.

"Thorn?" she asked in a shaky voice.

"When we woke up after the dream, you did not want to finish what we had started."

"I was afraid."

"Of me?"

Her fists clenched and unclenched at her sides as she thought of what was at stake. "Of taking risks. Of trusting my feelings."

"And now?"

Now she was lost. Lost without him. Trapped in a world between fantasy and reality. Yet he could be hers...if she dared.

She held out her hand to him.

He came to her, stepping under the pink light, the molecules dancing over his skin like a tiny meteor shower.

She said his name again. This time with more confidence.

He reached to touch her, sliding his fingers over her ribs the way she'd done to him, making her exhale a long sigh of pleasure.

"You do not know me." His voice was low and full of pain. "I have no right to touch you intimately. No right to drag you into my problems. I should tell you things—"

She stopped him by pressing her fingers to his lips. "Later. For now I know everything that's important."

His eyes held a challenge and a question. "Lift your hands over your head."

Did he know that was a gesture of surrender?

She did as he asked, and he followed the length of her arms with his fingertips, reaching up to her wrists, where he pressed his fingers against the pounding pulse points.

She dragged in a shuddering breath, but she made no move to pull away.

"Ah, you do trust me," he murmured. "Even after everything that has happened."

She heard the deep feeling in his voice. "Heart and soul."

He held her gaze as he reached back to a panel beside the door. The pink light faded. The molecules no longer danced and swirled around them. Now the tiny chamber was a dimly lit, intimate place.

"I do not want you to feel any sensation against your body but my touch," he growled as his fingertips played over the soft skin of her inner arms, then paused to caress the sensitive hollows at their base. She hadn't known they were erogenous zones. But she felt her body catch fire as he pressed and stroked her there.

"Only you," she breathed, bracing her palms against the walls. "That's all I want."

He stepped back a little, his hands going to her hair, fluffing it out around her head.

"A golden cloud," he murmured, combing through the soft strands. "So beautiful. I wish I had more words in your language to tell you how deeply you affect me."

"You don't need words," she whispered.

His eyes deepened to midnight blue as he cupped her breasts in his hands. "You are magnificent. Like no other woman."

His words brought a rush of pleasure. He smiled and, with teasing little strokes, began to caress her so that her nipples hardened to tight, exquisitely sensitive buds. Then he began to draw circles that came closer and closer to those points of sensation without touching them.

"Please," she begged. "Please."

"This?"

"Oh, yes."

"And this?" He scoured her with his roughened fingertips, making her insides liquefy.

"Oh!"

Head back, breath coming in little gasps, she stood before him as his fingers moved over her body in tiny sensual patterns she'd never dreamed of, and his lips played with her neck, the edge of her jaw and finally the coral buds he had brought to throbbing peaks of pleasure. She had only limited experience with men. But she sensed that this one was an extraordinary lover. He seemed to know every erotic secret of a woman's body.

His face was intense, his navy eyes catching every nuance of her response and heightening her delight a thousandfold.

"This is better than any dream," she gasped out.

"Oh, yes."

When she reached for him, he stopped her hands.

"Let me touch you," she begged. "I want to give you the same pleasure you're giving me."

He shook his head. "I have been alone for a long time. Do you understand?"

"Yes."

But it was impossible for her to remain entirely submissive. When his lips nibbled at hers, she cried his name and angled her head to deepen the kiss. When his hands stroked down her belly and through the triangle of hair at its base, she whimpered and moved against him.

His fingers drifted lower, finding her liquid core, stroking with a knowing finesse that made her gasp as little shock waves coursed through her. And all the time he spoke to her, low intimate words, sometimes in English, sometimes in his own language.

"Thorn. Please. I need...you," she gasped.

"Put your hands on my shoulders, *dubina.*"

She did, and he lifted her up. She hadn't known there was a little shelf in the wall behind her until he set her onto it.

Heat curled in her stomach as he moved between her knees. She instinctively braced her feet against the curved walls. She was utterly open to him, utterly vulnerable, and she looked up boldly into his blue eyes.

They held her, burning into her soul. Yet she saw the same defenselessness she felt. Then he thrust forward into her body, joining his flesh with hers, and she called out his name as he filled her.

Instinctively she began to rock against him, but he stopped her with urgent hands on her hips, his chest rising and falling in ragged gasps.

"No. Be still, sweet. Be very still."

Every fiber of her being bade her to drive for completion. But she did as he asked. For long moments he stood with his eyes closed, breathing deeply, his face tight as he fought for control. Then he brushed his lips back and forth against hers while he cupped her breasts once more, running his thumbs over the centers, caressing her in wonderfully erotic ways that brought waves of shuddering sensation sweeping over her body.

Her inner muscles contracted around him, making them both gasp.

She couldn't hold back a whimper as one of his hands moved to the place where their bodies were joined, stroking a rhythm that built her tension to a peak almost beyond endurance.

"Let me. Thorn, let me," she pleaded.

"Yes!"

Her hips moved in frantic spasms. "Thorn!" She cried his name again as she toppled over the edge, her fingers digging into his shoulders as shock after shock of pure pleasure took her. He drove into her, finally, with powerful strokes that pushed her against the wall. And then he threw his head back in a hoarse shout that echoed in the tiny chamber.

Cassie slumped against him, sated. Thorn kissed the damp hair that clung to her cheek.

She raised her hands enough to languidly stroke the slick muscles of his back.

He turned slightly, reaching behind him, and she felt the refreshing tingle of the molecules against her skin again.

She rested her head against his shoulder and for

long moments they drifted in the contented afterglow, his arms strong and secure around her.

"We cannot stay here forever," he finally said.

She sighed and nodded, slipping off the shelf and bracing her hands on his shoulders as she stood.

He turned off the chamber and led her out. Instead of the shirt and pants he'd selected earlier, he brought her a sleep raiment and helped her into the sleeves.

"Now you are all covered up. Modest."

She blushed and he stroked her cheek.

"So lovely."

His face held a mixture of warmth and something she was afraid to examine too closely. She sensed there were things he wanted to say, perhaps things she didn't want to hear.

But she needed to cling to the wonderful feeling of closeness.

"Sleep with me," she murmured.

"There is much I need to tell you."

She watched his internal debate. When he turned and picked up the smoke-drenched clothes from the floor and shoved them into a hidden wall slot, she felt a knot of uncertainty grow in her stomach.

When he finished, she took his hand. "Are you going to tell me you regret making love to me?" she managed to ask.

"Never!"

"Then whatever you want to say can wait until the morning."

She held her breath during his thirty-second pause.

"All right."

Cassie felt as if she'd won a monumental victory. Turning, she led him back to the bedroom. He unfastened the top of the covers from the headboard, and she slipped onto the wide bunk. He came down beside her, and she snuggled into his warmth. Moments later, the lights dimmed to a gentle glow near the door of the grooming alcove.

She turned and held him to her, and his arms went around her. His lips nibbled along her hairline, found her ear and did things that sent an erotic shiver sizzling through her body.

She let the sensations carry her along. There was so much she wanted to say, reassuring things. But she wasn't going to risk starting a discussion that she didn't know if she could finish. And she knew he must feel the same way. Tears misted her eyes, but she blinked them back. Thoughts of the future were dangerous. It was safer to dedicate herself simply to enjoying the night they had together.

CASSIE DIDN'T KNOW when Thorn awoke. When her eyes blinked open, she found him standing by the bed and gazing down at her with a tender expression.

"How do you feel?"

She stretched luxuriously. "Wonderful."

"I should have let you get more sleep."

"It's quality, not quantity, that counts."

His face turned serious. "Are we talking about sleeping or making love?"

She felt her cheeks grow rosy. "I meant sleeping."

"And the other? Did I make too many demands last night?"

"Never." She'd never dreamed of such sensuality or such rapture. Nor was she accustomed to talking about her feelings. But she struggled to come up with words that would capture the night. "Loving you was the most breathtaking thing that ever happened to me. You made me feel exhilarated and cherished.''

''Yes. That is a good description of how it was for me.''

They smiled into each other's eyes. When she held out her hand, he settled on the edge of the bed. Then she noticed he was holding two cups from which a delicious smell wafted.

She drew in the heady scent. ''What is it?''

''We call it ambrosia.''

''Food for the gods.''

''What?''

''That's what the ancient Greeks said their gods ate.''

He looked momentarily startled. ''I hope it lives up to the advance notices.''

Cassie started to sit up, remembered she'd cast off her sleep raiment soon after getting into bed and dragged the covers up around her breasts.

''Modest, as always,'' Thorn teased.

She ignored him and took a small sip. The beverage was delectable. Like fruit and wine but with tastes she couldn't identify.

''Do you like it?''

''You had *this,* and you let me fix dehydrated chicken soup?''

''I did not know what things I would find here, *dubina.*''

''What does that word mean?''

''It is a very small, very beautiful white bird. Rare and precious. So it translates into 'dear one.''' He paused for several heartbeats. ''On my...in my land.''

She felt the room had suddenly become rife with tension. And she admitted what she had been fighting to deny during their glorious night of lovemaking. She'd gathered all her courage and made a decision last night, and a door to untold riches had opened before her. Yet it could slam shut again, unless Thorn trusted her.

Fear shimmered through her like an icy rain penetrating her to the marrow of her bones. Struggling to appear calm, she found his hand and folded it into hers. "You want to tell me where you come from?"

"A long way from here."

"Well the cold war's over, so I guess you're not a Russian spy," she quipped. "Unless they groomed you for a special mission and forgot about you. Is that your secret?"

"What is a Russian spy?"

She laughed. "I think we're in serious trouble. You and I."

His face was regretful. Sad. "We should have talked before I let myself get carried away."

Cassie fought to keep her voice steady. "You said you have children. What about your wife?" she managed to ask. "Is she the problem between us?"

He gave a little shake of his head. "It was over between me and Sanda a long time ago."

Cassie let out the breath she was holding.

For several moments Thorn seemed lost in memories—good and bad. Then he began to speak. "She and I met when we were young and both working on field projects. After the twins were born, she was restless living in the city and wanted to go back to our old life. I argued that we needed to give Reah and Januk more stability." He sighed. "She tried to give the three of us what we needed, I think. But I knew she was unhappy, and our relationship was falling apart. Finally I told her to go ahead and take a short assignment away from home. I was hoping we could work a compromise where she would be with us part of the time."

He paused, and Cassie saw the anguish etched into his features. "She was coming home on leave. But there was a flier crash," he said in a gritty voice. "Everybody on board was killed."

"I'm sorry," Cassie whispered, finding his hand and gripping it tightly.

"I should have—"

"Don't beat yourself up about her decisions."

Thorn nodded, although she suspected he was never going to stop blaming himself.

"And now Reah and Januk have ended up completely alone," he grated. "In the care of strangers."

"Perhaps with loving strangers," Cassie murmured. "A couple who wanted children and couldn't have any of their own. People who will take good care of the girl and boy fate gave them. But even so, Reah and Januk never will forget their father."

He was hanging on her words, she saw, trying to make himself believe they were true, and she struggled to give him as much comfort as she could.

"Thorn, I know you were a good parent," she said. "If I'd had even a little time with someone like you, I would have been—" She swallowed, wishing she hadn't started down this avenue.

"Been what?"

"Happier," she said in a low voice. "Better adjusted, as the psychologists say."

"Cassie." He took her in his arms, and they held each other, rocking slightly, giving and taking comfort.

Finally, he drew away, putting several inches of space between them. "I think I am only going to add to your problems."

She shook her head violently.

"You may not like the rest of what I am going to tell you."

She held his hand tightly, unwilling to relinquish the contact of his flesh against hers.

"You may think I am lying," he continued. "Or suffering from...delusions."

"You're wrong. I've told you already, I know the important things about you."

"You know very little."

"I know you're an honorable man. You're strong willed." She gave a little laugh. "Arrogant. And stubborn. But you're good. On a very fundamental level. I know you have deep convictions that frightened a man named Lodar, so he exiled you to this secret place." She swallowed. "I've been trying to figure out where you come from. There are a couple of possibilities."

He waited, watching her with unnerving attention.

She continued in a matter-of-fact voice that she hoped hid the tension twisting inside her. "I suppose it's conceivable that there's an advanced civilization somewhere on earth that we don't know about. Under the ocean—the lost city of Atlantis—or deep underground. But I think it's more likely that you're from the future. And Lodar shoved you into a time machine and sent you back to our era."

"A time machine," Thorn echoed. "You have come up with a logical explanation for my presence here. In a way, you are right. Yet not precisely accurate."

Cassie felt a shiver run over her skin. "What, then?"

"Lodar stuffed me into a sleeping chamber. Well, not exactly sleep in the normal sense of the word. Something deeper. Where the body's processes are slowed—virtually stopped. My people use it for long journeys."

"I don't understand."

"I think your entering the station activated an automatic process that woke me up. Until then, I was in suspended animation. I did the calculations while you were recovering from the fire. I had been sleeping for..." He stopped and swallowed, then continued in a flat voice. "Two thousand, eight hundred and fifty-five years."

Cassie gasped. "That...that's impossible."

His mouth twisted. "I would have agreed. To my knowledge, nobody has ever survived that long a timespan in a delta cylinder." He held out his hands, turning them palms up. "But it appears to be true."

"But that means... Are you telling me there was a highly advanced civilization on earth thousands of years ago? Why haven't archaeologists discovered some evidence?"

"Cassie," he said very gravely. "Are there stories in your mythology about men coming from the sky in strange ships? Men from another world?"

As he spoke, the blood drained from her face.

"That frightens you," he said in a flat voice.

She clung to his hand again, feeling the solid bones beneath his warm flesh. Scooting closer, she pressed against his shoulder.

"Thorn—"

"Do you believe me?" he asked sharply. "That I

am not from your world. That my people visited here long ago?"

"Some people tell stories about being abducted by aliens *now,*" she whispered. "There are books about it. Movies. Television programs. But the aliens don't look like you. They're supposed to be small and pale with big eyes."

"Ah, how the mighty have fallen!"

Cassie laughed. Then her expression sobered again. "Thorn, I've had clues all along that you were extraordinary. Still it's hard to believe that a man from another..."

"Galaxy," he supplied.

"Another galaxy could look so much like us." She gazed into his crystal blue eyes as she stroked her fingers over his cheek, brushing back and forth against the scratchy surface of his beard. He sat very still, watching her gravely. Only his lips moved against her fingertips as she softly touched them.

She tunneled her hand through the thick hair of his chest and couldn't stop herself from brushing across his nipples. His little indrawn breath brought a knowing thrill. Whatever else might be true, he was a man, a man who responded to her on a very basic level.

She found his hand again and meshed the fingers with his, holding them up for him to see. "You and I fit together as if it were meant to be," she murmured. Passion flared in his eyes, and she knew he had understood her meaning perfectly. "You may have come from far away," she added, "but the things you want from life, the things you feel, are like ours."

They remained silent for several moments. "My people thought it strange, too, that your race was so similar to ours. We had traveled so far to get here, and we were prepared for anything.'' He laughed. ''Before our first expedition left, our most advanced scientists wrote scholarly articles about how we might meet with intelligent insects or reptiles or beings with crystalline rock structure. So it was a shock to meet the dominant life-forms here. We did genetic studies and discovered that your people and ours must have common roots. That somehow, in a time long ago, the universe was seeded with the ancestors of humankind.''

Cassie nodded. It was difficult to take in the scope of what he was saying, but his calm, rational voice helped keep her anchored.

''But when we arrived, your civilization was in a very primitive stage of development. People like Lodar were delighted with the disparity. He enjoyed showing off the wonders of our technology.'' Thorn's voice turned hard. ''He especially enjoyed frightening the natives and taking advantage of their superstitions. That is how I got into trouble. I was sent here to gather information for the High Council on what he was doing. I should have kept my mouth shut until I got back home. But I could not watch his antics.''

''You brought your children with you?''

''It was the only way to keep our family together. The journey from my world to yours took thirty years, with the crew and passengers in suspended animation. If I had left Reah and Januk at home, they would have been old by the time I returned.''

She nodded slowly. ''It's a lot to deal with. I'm having trouble absorbing it all.''

''Then you know how I felt when I woke up. I thought that either Lodar had stranded me in another time or that he was still here—and using you to get evidence to convict me of some crime."

The mixture of emotions on his face made her heart squeeze. "No wonder you were afraid to trust me." Blindly she reached for him, clasping him to her breast. His arms came up to circle her shoulders. Their strength was reassuring. Turning her head, she pressed her face against his neck, feeling the strong, steady pulse. He was flesh and blood, a man. A man who was both commanding and vulnerable, powerful and wounded. And he had traveled unimaginably far in time and space. That single fact should change everything, yet it did not. Perhaps it was the very reason she'd been drawn to him.

She could feel his tension as he waited for her to say something more. Lifting her head, she met his troubled gaze.

"Where you come from doesn't alter anything between us."

"It has to."

"No. Because I already know you very well," she murmured. "Know you and trust you."

He gazed at her in wonder as he combed his fingers through her hair. "Of all the people on your planet, I still cannot believe you were the one who found me."

"You called me here. In your dreams," she murmured.

"Dreams can be a powerful form of communication for my people. Usually it happens when a man and a woman—" He stopped abruptly.

"When a man and a woman what?"

"Are very close."

A tiny exclamation escaped from her throat, and her hands tightened convulsively on his shoulders.

"But I never heard of it happening like this," he said emphatically. "Physical joining comes first. Then shared dreams. Not the other way around. And it does not necessarily happen—even with couples who have been mated for years."

She nodded gravely, swamped by the implications. She and Thorn had reached a level of intimacy that few could achieve.

He was still speaking. "I do not know how I reached a woman I had never even touched. Maybe that is why there was such an unreal quality to those earlier dream meetings. Because we had never seen each other in actual life. Never met. But I had no right to drag you into my problems," he added with sudden conviction.

"You didn't drag me into anything."

"Then what?" he challenged.

"You were the one man in all the world I trusted."

He shook his head in disbelief.

"Do you know how I ended up coming here? I was at the State Department—"

"The what?"

"A government agency that deals with foreign countries. I take special assignments for them, and my boss, Victor Kirkland, wanted to offer me an easy two weeks in Europe, as a reward for past performance. But all the time we were sitting in his office talking about exciting locales in France and Italy, my eyes kept flicking to a folder on his desk. I wanted to pick it up so badly that my fingers were actually tingling."

She lowered her gaze momentarily. "When Victor was called out of the room, I did something I've never done in my life. Ever. I violated his professional privacy and opened the folder.

"It was a report by another government agency—the Federal Communications Commission—about a strange energy source emanating from the Alaskan wilderness. The reason Victor had the information was that our satellites had discovered a similar energy signature at an archeological site in eastern Europe. The FCC was planning to investigate the domestic location. They wanted Victor to get someone on the team, excavating the foreign locale."

Thorn's attention was riveted to her. "Where?" he demanded.

"Greece."

"I do not know the name."

"It's in the part of the world you were looking at—on the globe from the television broadcast."

"How far away is it?"

"A long way. Maybe seven thousand miles."

His eyes narrowed. "Maybe that is too far."

She wasn't following his logic. But she wanted to finish the story, so he'd understand her motives. "I put the folder down before Victor caught me. I told him I'd think about the job offer he'd made. But when I left his office, I went straight to a telephone and called a high-level contact I have at the FCC. She owed me a favor, so I gave her a story about needing to combine my travel agency with my government jobs and asked her to recommend me for the Alaska assignment.

"But I didn't stop there. I felt strongly about coming here. And I kept doing things that were completely out of character. I also called Victor and reminded him that my sister, Marissa, was arrested while she was working for him. And I'd been the one who organized her rescue. I told him I'd heard he was working with the FCC, and he could settle the score with us by getting me the Alaskan job. I've never made that kind of demand before. I've never felt a compulsion to travel to a particular location. I think if Victor hadn't helped, I would have come up here by myself. Because I knew something important was waiting for me. Now I know it was you."

They stared at each other for an endless space of time.

"Cassie," he whispered. "It would be better for you if you had not come to this place."

She raised her head so that she could meet his eyes. "It was my choice."

"Not when I compelled your presence."

Frustration clogged her throat. "Haven't you listened to a thing I've said? It was something *I* wanted. I wanted to know you in real life—not just in dreams."

"I am a man without a past. Without a means of making a living. And I have knowledge that could be dangerous to the stability of your world."

She wouldn't let him continue that argument. "I know what's happened to you seems overwhelming. But I have a whole group of friends who can help us. Like Jason Zacharias and my brother-in-law, Jed Prentiss. They have all kinds of contacts in the intelligence community—people who can manufacture an identity for you—so you won't have to reveal who you are unless you want to. They can get you a birth certificate, a driver's license, a social security card and all the other credentials that will make it look like you were born in the Black Hills of South Dakota, if that's where we pick."

Her mind raced, and ideas tumbled from her lips. "South Dakota's probably a good choice, because you look like a Native American. I know our culture's complicated. But you're a quick study. It won't take long for me to teach you—"

He cut her off with a gruff exclamation in his own language.

She took him roughly by the shoulders. "Thorn, I know you're staggered by what Lodar did to you. Anyone would have trouble coping with a society where everything is new and strange. But don't you see? You have to make the best of it. You have to fit yourself into my world—make a contribution. It's the only way to cheat Lodar of his victory."

"I may not get the chance."

The tone of his voice sent a cold chill sweeping across her skin. "What do you mean? You can make a future for yourself. You know so much. You'll have so much to contribute—"

"You do not understand!" His tone was harsh, his eyes flinty. They stopped her words and sent prickles across her flesh. "Cassie, my future may be limited...."

She struggled to keep her voice steady. "How limited?"

"A few days."

Chapter Eight

Cassie's fingers locked on Thorn's naked shoulders. They were strong and reassuringly solid. "What... what do you mean?" she managed to ask.

"I may not have much time. It depends on how fast we can get to the place you call Greece."

"Why?"

"Lodar left me a vaccine I must take. But I do not know whether it was safeguarded as securely as the delta cylinder."

Cassie stared at him, trying to take it all in. "You're going too fast for me. What vaccine?"

"There were several expeditions from my planet that landed here—over a period of fifty of your years. When the first team came, some of them became seriously ill and died. Our healers discovered that we had no immunity to certain bacteria in your soil. So they devised a vaccine. I had one dose. It takes two injections for full immunity. I was due for a second when Lodar kidnapped me."

Cassie nodded, denying her panic. "The hiding place is probably as well protected as you were."

He shook his head. "I do not know. There are many prohibitions in our society about taking a human life. So it appears that even a man as dishonorable as Lodar could not simply kill me to rid himself of a nagging problem. That was why he left me here. Probably he was hoping things would go wrong.

"Like the fire. It was not *exactly* planned. But I did some investigating while you were asleep. He made a mistake in the computer instructions that caused the projector to dangerously overheat. He could have done the same thing with the vaccine storage system—without admitting to himself what he was thinking. Or that archaeological team in Greece could have broken into the storage site."

"No!" Cassie refused to imagine the problem couldn't be solved. "Even if we don't find the vaccine, we have other options. I know you think of my people as primitive, but medical science has made amazing progress in the past few years. Another one of my friends, Katie Martin, is a doctor who specializes in developing new drugs. She and her husband, Mac McQuade, travel all over the world, finding medicinal plants and turning them into useful medicines. Maybe they can synthesize a vaccine from your own blood. Or use some kind of genetic engineering technique to manufacture more."

"Maybe." Thorn sounded doubtful.

She plowed on as a new idea struck her. "And if it's going to take some time to refine the process, we could put you back to sleep in the delta cylinder."

He shook his head. "That is not an option. I also did a diagnostic on the cylinder. After so many years of continuous operation, its functions were starting to degrade. At first it kept me deeply asleep. But finally the mechanism allowed me to rise to a higher level of consciousness."

"And you could dream?" Cassie asked. "That's how you were able to call me?"

"Yes."

"So that was an advantage!"

"In one way. But the cylinder would not have kept working much longer."

Cassie felt a tremor go through her. Slipping her arms around Thorn's back, she pulled him close and held on tight. Her face pressed into the thick hair of his chest, and her lips moved against his skin. "I'm glad I got here in time."

"Perhaps you did," he whispered, almost as if he were speaking against his will.

She knew that after everything he'd been through, he couldn't dare trust in a happy ending. But she wasn't going to let him give up hope. "We'll go right to Greece," she promised. "As soon as we break out of here. You said you took an inventory of the station's supplies. Did you find any digging implements?"

"Not precisely. But there is portable heating equipment that I think we can use to melt a passage through the snow."

She sprang off the bed. "Then let's do it. I'm not cleared for instrument flying, so I'd like to make it back to Anchorage before it gets dark."

Thorn retrieved her clothing from the slot in the grooming alcove. Every item was spotless and smelled as if it had been hanging on a clothesline in the crisp mountain air.

While she dressed, Thorn searched through the supplies and found himself silver boots that were a reasonable fit. He also came up with a silver-colored jacket.

Cassie eyed him doubtfully. "I wish we had more conventional clothes for you," she mused.

"I will stand out in a crowd?"

"Not for long. We'll go straight from the airport to a clothing store."

"I have been thinking about what you said. This scheme of yours is not going to be as easy as you assume," Thorn muttered.

"What scheme?"

"Passing me off as one of your people."

"We'll manage."

"I assume the airplane belongs to your guide. When you come home without him, you are going to have to make some explanation to the authorities."

"I'll tell the truth. What happened to Glen isn't my fault."

"Yes, but will they want to investigate? What is going to happen when they find this installation that you thought was so strange? Your military will be all over the place, taking samples and conducting tests. They will question you about exactly what you did here. And they will ask about me."

Cassie nodded gravely. As soon as the Defense Department got wind of a hidden base under an Alaskan mountain, they'd want to know how it got there. "You're right, but we can be in hiding by then," she argued. "I told you, my friends will help us."

Thorn sighed. "Two thousand years ago, your people marveled at our technology. They thought we were gods and began making up stories about our awesome deeds."

"We're hardly at the same level."

"I know that. But the dangers are greater. I watched your television. You look like us, but some of your traits are different. On my planet, there was only one government. You have many nations—some warring with one another. We ended war long ago. We do not kill each other. You live in a violent world where your entertainment media celebrate murder, where governments and individuals seek ways to gain power over one another. What if someone sees me as a threat? Suppose they decide I have come here to take over the world? Then it would be dangerous for you to associate with me."

"Television gives a distorted picture. We're not all bad," Cassie retorted. Yet he'd started her thinking about movies like *The Day the Earth Stood Still* and *Star Man* where the authorities welcomed a visitor from another planet with machine guns.

Thorn touched her cheek with his knuckle and stroked across her lips. "Some of you are very warm and generous. Very loving," he said quietly. "Some of you would come to the aid of a stranger."

She swallowed hard.

"I am sorry to make you worry about things I may not fully understand."

"No. There are plenty of people who would be afraid of you. Or they might think they could use your power."

Thorn looked thoughtful. "Then I must hide this place. There are explosive charges included with the supplies. We could set blasts that would bury the entrance to the installation under rock. Then when your authorities come looking for evidence, they will find only the avalanche."

"And I could explain your coming back with me by saying you were out here camping," Cassie finished. "And your camping equipment was buried under the avalanche that trapped me."

"That might work," Thorn mused.

Cassie wasn't sure whether he believed the statement or whether he was simply trying to be reassuring. But she was determined to pull off the plan. "Or maybe we'd better fly to a small airport near the city—where they don't even know Glen. That way we'll get a head start."

"There are a few things I should take with me. Some of the healing patches. Equipment to detect the cache in Greece. Other supplies that might be useful."

"I'll help you pack."

As Thorn checked the provisions, made selections and filled carry packs, they talked quietly. By mutual agreement, they stayed away from heavy topics. Mostly Cassie tried to prepare him for what he would see when they reached Anchorage.

"It's the biggest city in Alaska. But small by most standards."

"How many people live there?"

"About two hundred and twenty-five thousand. But in summer there are lots of tourists—people who come here because the state is so wild and beautiful. The city's very clean and neat. There are flower baskets hanging from the light poles in the shopping area. And spectacular flower displays in the parks. The plants grow huge in summer because there's so much daylight."

She couldn't believe she was babbling on about flowers. But she kept talking, relating the tour guide information that popped into her head, knowing it was a way of trying to cope with her building tension.

Now that Thorn had raised so many questions, she knew she wasn't going to feel secure until the two of them were back in Baltimore where they could call on her friends for help.

She didn't know she and Thorn were already being stalked.

THE MOMENT the helicopter landed on the private island near Sicily, Feydor Lenov was ushered into a limousine and rushed to his employer's heavily guarded estate. He knew the VIP reception wasn't for him, but for what he carried in his protective cases. His eyes swept nervously around the leather interior of the car, stopping at the fully stocked bar. He could use a glass of vodka before he met Montague. How would the man react when he found out that some of the merchandise was in less than perfect condition?

Jacques Montague had gotten permission for the dig from the Greek government with the understanding that any artifacts would remain within the country. But he'd had no intention of honoring the agreement. Instead, he'd ordered Feydor to bring anything of significance directly to him. The man who'd stolen the tablets from Zeke Chambers fingered the handle of a padded steel case. Perhaps he was overreacting. Maybe when the billionaire saw the tablets, he'd reward the messenger with a generous bonus.

Inside Montague's mansion, Feydor had a quick impression of Italian marble floors, a glittering chandelier worthy of a czar's palace and framed Cezannes and Chagalls on cream-colored walls. A servant led him down a hall into the library. In the center was a glass case displaying a gold-trimmed hand-scribed copy of the Koran. The Russian stepped toward it, but a cough from behind made him freeze and then turn.

A short man with dark hair and a mustache stood framed in the doorway. It was Montague. Despite his slender build, he radiated energy and authority. Although Lenov had been "acquiring" priceless artifacts for the billionaire for more than ten years, he'd only met Jacques Montague once. Their business was usually conducted on the phone, via fax, or through intermediaries. But he'd never forgotten the man's cold black eyes. Those same eyes focused on him like a coroner performing an autopsy.

"You've brought the merchandise?" Montague's voice was sharp and authoritative as ever.

"Yes. Everything's in those cases," Lenov replied, pointing to the heavy steel lockers two servants were carrying in. When they had left the room, Feydor bent down and opened the lock. "This is what Zeke Chambers and Marie Pindel found in the cave."

Reverently Montague lifted the protective covering from a tablet. "*Oui,* I was right," he said almost to himself. "You brought everything?"

The Russian nodded. Carefully he unwrapped the vases and pitchers that were found at the site and placed them on the desk.

Lenov held his breath as Montague inspected the treasure. He paused over a small bottle. "This one's *ruined.* How did this happen?"

"I don't know. Perhaps the American did it," the Russian offered, trying to keep the tremors out of his voice. He'd heard rumors of how Montague dealt with incompetence.

"That doesn't sound like Chambers. He's very

careful. That's why I agreed to having him on the dig."

Lenov waited for what seemed like centuries, while Montague examined the bottle.

"Perhaps the explosion we used to uncover the inner chamber damaged it."

"Yes," Lenov agreed eagerly.

"Too bad. But we won't let this set us back. Chambers is on to something important with the tablets. I can feel it. He's gone back to Washington to question Kirkland. I want you to follow Chambers and bring me back whatever he discovers. My private plane and pilot are at your disposal. Charge anything you need to my account. But don't disappoint me." With those orders, he turned and marched out.

Lenov sighed. Instead of a reward for work well done, he'd drawn another assignment. Getting the jump on Zeke Chambers a second time was going to be extremely difficult. He just hoped it wasn't impossible.

WHEN THORN HAD CHECKED the supplies, he and Cassie returned to the analyzer console where he issued several commands.

Then he turned to her. "I must shut down all functions of the station so that the power will not be detected from outside. Are you ready?"

She nodded tightly and moved to stand with her shoulder pressed to his.

With a few additional instructions to the analyzer, he turned off every system—including life support, heat and light.

Immediately, the room was plunged into impenetrable blackness.

"We must work quickly," he told her as he switched on the first of two large torches that were much like high-powered flashlights, only the beams were considerably wider. "Because the ventilators are no longer recycling the air."

"I...know..."

He heard the quaver in her voice, knew the blackness made her nervous as a tree cat in sunlight. He hadn't told her it was going to be risky melting their way through the snow. In fact, he was determined not to let his own tension show. He knit his fingers with hers and squeezed tightly. "Okay?"

"Yes," she told him, obviously fighting to make her voice sound steady. At the end of the tunnel, they stepped out into the snow cave. Cassie held one of the lights while he played a scanner over the barrier.

At first, he felt his own alarm grow. The wall was thick, thicker than he'd expected. He moved down the enclosure. Finally, the readings changed. Better. But not optimal. However, it was the best he could do.

"It is thinner here." He pointed to an area that looked exactly like the rest.

"How do you know?"

"This instrument can perform the measurement with low-level broadcast waves." He pocketed the meter, bent over one of the portable heaters and attached a nozzle to the outlet. Then he snapped a power pack into place. In the confines of the cave, the noise of the blower was like being inside the drive room of an ancient watercraft.

"Sorry," he shouted, making an adjustment that built the roar even louder. Then he wished himself good fortune and pointed the nozzle at the spot where he'd determined the distance to the outside was shortest. Immediately, a hole opened in the snow.

He let out the breath he'd been holding. So far, so good. Moving forward, he kept the nozzle aimed at the cavity. Water dropped from the ceiling and sides, some of it turning to steam, and he was forced to pause every few minutes to see what was happening.

On the third break, he cut off the machine and wiped sweat from his forehead.

"Do you want me to take a turn?" Cassie asked.

"No." He wasn't going to tell her it was too dangerous.

Cassie moved forward and shone the light along the edge of the opening. It glistened on a crust of ice. Good. It would stabilize the surface.

The ice extended down a rounded tunnel about four feet wide and about ten feet long. But it still ended in a solid wall of white.

"If it's thin here, I hate to think about the thick part," she murmured.

"A relative term." Avoiding her eyes, Thorn crouched and started to move forward into the passageway he'd created.

Cassie grabbed his shoulder. "How do you know it's safe?"

He sighed. "I do not. But there is no choice. The blast from the heater is ineffective beyond this range."

Before she could muster an objection, he started down the tunnel. In a moment he sensed her coming in behind him.

"Go back to the entrance."

"Why?"

"If the tunnel collapses, you will have to use the other machine to get me out."

He saw the fear in her eyes. She masked it with a sharp retort. "Then you'd better show me how it works."

"All right." He stopped his forward progress long enough to demonstrate which settings to press.

She nodded tensely.

He gave her arm a quick squeeze before inching forward again, aiming the nozzle straight ahead. The machine roared. This time, in addition to dripping water, small piles of snow began coming down from the ceiling. The first time, he jumped back expecting the ceiling to give way. When nothing bigger fell, he kept moving.

Despite his warning, Cassie came farther into the tunnel than he'd like, training the beam on the end of the nozzle. She was like no other woman he'd met. On his own world or on hers. She'd been terrified when she was buried under the snow, yet she was taking that risk again, to help him see what he was doing.

He hated putting her in danger. But he silently admitted he needed all the help he could get. Gritting his teeth, he pushed forward, trying not to doubt his initial scanner readings.

He longed to stop and wipe away the water on his face. But he kept going, because the longer the weight of the snow pressed down on the tunnel, the more dangerous it would become. He was about twelve feet up the tunnel when he paused again and gave a little shout of victory. Cassie scooted up behind him as he shut off the blower. Taking her arm, he ushered her into what seemed like deafening silence.

The sunlight was momentarily blinding. Covering his eyes, he drew in several deep breaths of fresh air.

Free. He was free.

Turning, he stared at the enormous cascade of snow from which they'd emerged. It started far up the mountain and covered several hundred feet of rock to their left and right. For the first time he understood the extent of Cassie's peril. What must it have been like to be standing out here when the snow came roaring down the mountain? Shuddering, he clasped her close.

"Glen couldn't get away," she whispered.

"I am glad you found the rock ledge."

"I'm glad I found you."

He nodded, trying to rein in his emotions as he breathed unfiltered air for the first time in centuries.

He wanted to throw back his head and shout. He wanted to perform an ancient dance of thanksgiving. But he was a man who never indulged in such displays. So he contented himself with closing his eyes and lifting his face to the sun.

The wind ruffled his hair as he gazed at the expanse of virgin wilderness with its stands of slender fir trees and craggy mountain ranges that stretched one behind the other into the distance. To the right and left, small waterfalls plummeted hundreds of feet down the sides of nearby cliffs.

"I visited much of your planet. But I could never have imagined a place like this. The land is very wild and open. And very beautiful," he said, his voice full of wonder as he took in the wilderness panorama.

"Imagine it in winter. When the temperature is forty degrees below freezing for weeks on end."

He and Cassie stood silently for several minutes, breathing the clean, cool air.

"I see why Lodar picked this location above others," he finally said. "It is isolated. Remote. We might be the only two people in the world."

"Civilization is as close as a two-hour flight."

Several large brown shapes drifted across a nearby slope.

"What are those?" he asked.

"Caribou, I think. Or maybe moose." She laughed. "I can't tell them apart for sure at this distance."

"Are they dangerous?"

"Not the caribou. A male moose might get aggressive and charge you in mating season."

"Which is?"

"Now."

"Then we will make sure not to disturb them. Are there other animals?"

"Ground squirrels. Dall sheep. Mountain goats. The wolves are hunters, but they mostly stay away from people. The bears are the biggest threat."

"They are meat eaters?"

"They eat everything from berries to fishermen. I hope you brought a gun in case we need it."

"Lodar left me no weapons. Did you come here... unarmed."

"Glen—my guide—had two rifles." She sighed. "He left one with the boat we used to get to shore. I guess we shouldn't hang around. Let's bring the supplies outside."

He turned and peered down the tunnel. "When everything is out, I can set the charges."

"I wish you didn't have to use explosives."

"I will be careful."

They were silent as they retraced their path down the passageway. Above them, the snow groaned and shifted. "This place isn't safe," she muttered.

He didn't voice his agreement, but he speeded up his pace.

When they'd ferried his small stock of necessities outside, he asked to borrow Cassie's watch. "I will set the charges with a fifteen-minute delay. That should give us plenty of time to get away."

Before going back in, he gave Cassie a reassuring hug that was meant to be quick. Instead, he held on to her for several long moments. Now that he was outside, it was almost impossible to make himself return to the cold, dark place where he'd been trapped for almost three thousand years. But the existence of the installation had to be hidden.

Cassie stood in the sunshine, listening to Thorn's footsteps recede. When he disappeared from view, her chest constricted. After a moment, she turned and stared at the slowly drifting clouds. Time inched past. Without her watch, she felt as if he'd been in there for hours.

Once more she thought she heard the snow shift above the tunnel.

"Thorn?" she called down the passage.

"I am finished with the charge."

"Thank God." The crunch of gravel made her pivot. Shading her eyes, she spotted a small blond animal gamboling up the slope toward her. For a moment she couldn't figure out what it could be, since the shape was wrong for a Dall sheep. Then she sucked in a quick breath as she realized it was a grizzly cub with the peculiar coloration of the region.

The youngster itself was more curious than dangerous. But Cassie knew that a bear cub was never far from its mother.

"Thorn!" she called urgently down the tunnel. "Hurry."

"What is wrong?" he answered, his voice reflecting the alarm in hers.

"I'm afraid we have company. Bears."

Before she could elaborate, the mother lumbered over the crest of the hill. Cassie's mouth went dry. The grizzly stared at her in surprise. Then the animal growled and reared onto its hind legs, its full nine-foot height and eight hundred pounds towering over Cassie like an avenging fury.

Chapter Nine

For a split second, Cassie considered ducking into the tunnel to escape from the angry bear. But that was a dangerous option. She and Thorn would both be trapped in the cave—with live explosives that were set to detonate in less than fifteen minutes.

"Cassie? What's wrong?" Thorn shouted, his footsteps hammering toward her.

"Can you defuse the charges?" she called.

"No."

"Damn. Stay back," she warned as the cub loped toward the tunnel entrance and stuck its head inside. Lord, what she wouldn't give for a rifle in her hand.

"Hey. Get away from there. Scat." Cassie waved her arms and bellowed to distract the nosy animal. Turning, the cub veered away from the passageway. But the youngster was the least of her problems. Bent on protecting her offspring, the mother charged forward, her gait deceptively clumsy. Teeth bared in an angry snarl, she hurtled directly at Cassie.

There was no time to think, only to act instinctively. As the animal reared and lunged, Cassie danced out of the way. But not quite fast enough.

Razor-sharp claws dug into the sleeve of her jacket, shredding the nylon fabric like tissue paper.

With a sob of terror, Cassie tried to duck away. But the animal stayed on the attack. This time Cassie wasn't so lucky. A set of needlelike scratches raked down the side of her cheek and tore into her left shoulder. Her scream of pain split the clear mountain air.

Behind her, the snow over the tunnel rumbled ominously. But she hardly heard. All her attention was focused on the bear as it wheeled and started for her once more, smelling her blood, coming in for the kill. Her shoulder throbbed. She could feel herself slowing down, knew that it was only a matter of time before the angry animal finished her off.

A horrified shout caught the grizzly off guard. *"Klat!"*

Both Cassie and the mother bear swung toward the new sound. In the next moment, Thorn barreled into the sunlight, blinking in the sudden brightness.

The whole equation shifted. The cub growled and retreated. The mother grizzly switched directions and made for the new threat.

"Get back! She can kill you with one swipe," Cassie screamed, swaying on her feet. With a burst of energy, she picked up a chunk of ice and hurled it at the animal's back. The effort sent her reeling, and she toppled heavily onto the ground.

The grizzly yelped and stopped in its tracks, leaning this way and that, as if it debated whether to go after the man who had just appeared or the woman who had hurled the ice ball.

"Cassie!" Thorn called, his voice hoarse with dread as he stared across the fifteen feet that separated them. He wouldn't get far with an eight-hundred-pound bear looming in his path.

"I'm all right," Cassie called out with as much conviction as she could muster.

Thorn's face was a mixture of anguish and frustration. "Your arm."

She turned her head and saw torn flesh and a bright splotch of her own blood. The red transformed itself into tiny spots dancing before her eyes. She knew she was going to faint, but somehow she held on to consciousness.

The bear started toward Thorn. "The heater," she gasped. "Blast it with the heater."

This time the grizzly swung toward the sound of her voice. She tried to push herself up and get out of the way. But she couldn't move more than a few inches.

She could hear Thorn cursing as he made for the equipment he'd dumped by the entrance to the cave. Rolling to her side, she tried to follow him with her eyes. Then the bear blocked her line of sight.

Cassie lay on the ground panting, watching the animal advance on her, eyes bright, teeth bared. Mustering one last surge of energy, Cassie braced against the ground. As the bear lunged, she raised her foot and kicked the animal's muzzle as hard as she could with the heel of her boot. Then she flopped back into the snow, her blood spreading in a wide patch around her.

The grizzly's howl of rage was accompanied by another sound—a roar that Cassie's fuzzy brain couldn't immediately identify. Then, with a jolt of recognition, she realized it was the heater. Louder than before.

The bear swung away from her. Then she saw Thorn, charging at the animal, the heater aimed in front of him like a machine gun. He'd turned up the power so high that the nozzle glowed red. A blast of super hot air hit the bear, and it howled and jumped back. Thorn kept advancing, his face savage, his eyes flashing fire.

The animal's fur began to singe. With a yelp of pain, the grizzly turned on its heels and galloped down the hill, the cub lumbering along behind.

Cassie fell back against the snow, hanging on to consciousness by sheer willpower. Thorn was at her side, leaning over her, examining her wounds, cursing.

She tried to reassure him with a squeeze of her fingers against his. It was too much effort, and she realized with the part of her mind that was still working that she must be in shock.

"The explosives... Got to...get you away from here. Quick."

He lifted her by the shoulders. She cried out in agony as he jostled her torn flesh.

"Sorry." He half lifted, half dragged her down the hill, away from the mound of snow that covered the installation.

The two packs of supplies he'd slung over his shoulder bounced against his body, partially blocking her view of the tunnel. But when she heard the massive pile shift, she raised her head. Over Thorn's shoulder she saw the entrance to the passageway cave in on itself. He spared a quick backward glance.

"Was that it?" she whispered.

"No. The tunnel gave out." Checking her watch, he picked up speed.

The rapid movement hurt terribly. Cassie pressed her face into Thorn's body and clung to him with her good arm. Waves of pain radiated from her shoulder. Gritting her teeth, she kept herself from crying out.

They were several hundred yards from the ruined entrance when she heard a rumble deep inside the snowbank. A split second later, the earth shook, and clumps of ice sprayed into the air like corn out of a giant popper.

Thorn eased her to the ground and crouched over her. Cassie sheltered her face against his chest. But he'd dragged her far enough away so that only a few of the frozen missiles landed around them.

Thorn waited until the ice storm ended. Then he switched his full attention to Cassie.

"I am sorry," he repeated.

"Not your fault," she managed to say with the last of her strength.

Taking off his jacket, he spread it on the ground and laid her on the silver fabric. When he gently examined her shoulder, she clamped her teeth together and closed her eyes.

Hot pain radiated down her arm to her hand, and she clenched the fingers. She supposed being able to move them was a good sign, since she'd heard of people who'd had an arm ripped completely off by a bear.

"It hurts. I know it hurts, *dubina,*" Thorn muttered, anguish making his voice rough.

Cassie lay very still. If she didn't move, the torn flesh didn't throb so badly. Part of her tried to float above the pain, yet she couldn't stop her thoughts from spinning on. They couldn't go back into the installation, and there was no way she could fly a plane in this condition. "Lord, what a mess," she whispered aloud.

Thorn bent over her, his face tense with strain. "Do not talk. I have something that will heal you."

Yanking the knapsacks off his shoulder, he fumbled inside and brought out several flat packets. Pulling off the outer layer, he pressed one to Cassie's shoulder and the other to her cheek.

She braced for a medicinal sting. Instead, a wonderful, soothing warmth seeped from the packet and into her body. The sensation was more apparent at the point of contact, but she felt it radiating outward, too, spreading through her system.

"Better?" he asked.

She sighed and nodded. Turning her head, she tried to look at her shoulder again.

"Be still. Let the compresses do their work." He found her hand and covered it with his.

For long moments, Cassie drifted, aware of little besides the clouds floating in the blue sky above her and the contact of Thorn's strong hand with hers. Sometime later, he lifted the compress from her cheek and gently touched the skin.

"It was not too deep. It is almost healed," he told her.

Her eyes flew open. "It can't be." Tentatively, she touched her face. To her amazement, when she patted the skin, she felt smooth tissue instead of deep claw marks. "What did you put on me?"

"A compound that regenerates damaged cells. Like when you were burned. Only this medication has more strength for injuries below the skin."

She flexed her arm. The shoulder still burned deep

inside, but she could tell that the wound was mending. "Does it prevent infection, too?"

"Of course."

She gave him a little smile. "Well, I think we've just solved the problem of how you're going to make a living in the brave new world."

"I am no healer."

"You don't have to be. My friends Katie and Mac have the credentials to market this compound. If you can go into business manufacturing it, you'll make a fortune."

"A lot of money?"

"Mm-hmm."

"Is that...ethical?"

"Why not?"

"I did not...develop it."

"Well, you didn't steal it, either. And it will be a tremendous benefit to humankind."

Cassie took in the serious expression on his face as he weighed the pros and cons of the suggestion. He wasn't a man who compromised his morality. But then, that was how he'd gotten into trouble in the first place. "There's nothing wrong with making a profit from your people's technology," she said.

"Perhaps."

"We'll talk more about it later." Cassie looked again at the place where the avalanche had tumbled down the mountain. "We can't stay here," she said.

"I know. But you lost some blood. And your body has suffered a massive shock. You must rest."

"For a little while," she conceded, snuggling against Thorn. He stroked the hair back from her face and bent to kiss her cheek, and she longed to feel the reassurance of his supple body pressed against the length of hers.

"Lie down with me," she whispered.

"I must sit up and keep watch. The bears could come back."

"Not those two," she argued. But she knew he was right. It would be foolish for both of them to let down their guard at the same time. "Give me half an hour."

"More, I think."

She closed her eyes and let the healing compress continue to do its work. The feeling it gave off was less intense now, but still very pleasant—like a heating pad easing a stiff muscle.

Sometime later she felt Thorn shift. Her eyes blinked open. With a little start, she realized she'd been sleeping deeply. Raising her head, she looked toward the sun and saw it had made considerable progress across the sky. "How long was I asleep?"

"Two of your hours."

"You should have wakened me sooner."

His hand lightly touched her cheek. She covered his fingers with hers. "You needed to mend."

"Again."

He looked regretful. "Consorting with me is hazardous to your health."

"Consorting! Where did you get that word?"

"Is it wrong?"

"Unusual, but I'm not going to let you sidetrack me. You didn't bring the bears. It was just bad luck they were in the area. If you hadn't driven them away, I'd be dead."

"Perhaps I am a magnet for bad luck."

"I predict your luck is going to change," she said, then laughed.

"What?"

"I just made one of those strange connections in my head. Do you know my name Cassie is short for Cassandra?"

"And?"

"Cassandra was important in Greek mythology. She was the daughter of the king of Troy, and she had the gift of knowing the future. But nobody ever believed her. And, uh, that led to disaster for her people."

"So I should trust in your judgment—and we will break the ancient curse?"

"Exactly."

Thorn gave her a little smile. "Perhaps you are a good-luck charm."

"I hope so." She sat up and inspected her shoulder. There were only faint red marks where the flesh had been torn. Gingerly she touched the skin. Miraculously, it was smooth and whole. "I think I'm ready to travel."

He scowled.

"Daylight won't last forever. Even this far north. We'd better start for the plane."

Thorn nodded tightly and helped her stand, watching her critically. Her first steps were wobbly. Still, she was awed at the speed of her recovery, considering that her shoulder had been ripped open only hours before.

"Which way?" he asked.

She pointed in the direction of the lake, and they started off at a very easy pace.

"How far?" he asked after about twenty minutes.

"A couple of miles."

Thorn's eyes narrowed with concern. "I wish you did not have to walk so far."

"I'll be all right."

In fact, she moved very slowly and had to stop and rest several times along the way. And she couldn't prevent herself from anxiously scanning the landscape for bears. None appeared.

Finally they made it to the shore. Cassie sat down on a flat rock, staring at the plane with relief as she caught her breath. It was large for a private aircraft, with a twelve-foot cargo area that could be converted for extra passengers. After a few minutes, she dragged herself to the overturned boat Glen had hidden behind some rocks. Inside was the extra rifle he'd decided to stash instead of carry.

"Now we're armed," she informed Thorn as she opened the barrel and checked the shells.

"The weapon fires deadly projectiles? Like on 'Bonanza'?"

"You're going to have to stop watching so many reruns."

While he examined the weapon, she surreptitiously wiped her sleeve across her brow. She felt a lot safer, but she wasn't so happy about how much energy their slow walk had used up. "After the fire, you took a stimulant. Do you have any more?" she asked Thorn.

"I cannot take more. It would be dangerous."

"I meant for me."

He shook his head. "The best thing is for your body to finish healing naturally."

"Thorn, I know you're a quick study. But I think I'm the one who's going to have to fly the aircraft. And that takes more energy than I have right now."

His answer was a low curse.

"As soon as we're safe, I'll go to bed for twenty-four hours. Or two days. Whatever you like." She gave him a wicked grin. "You can hold me captive there."

He fought to keep from returning the smile. "We were talking about rest. Healing."

"Mmm."

He rolled his eyes. "Cassie, if I give you the stimulant, you must promise to be cautious."

"How?"

"The drug is powerful. You may not be prepared for the way you will react. You will feel confident. Physically strong. It could affect your judgment."

"Forewarned is forearmed."

Still, he hesitated, and he continued to look reluctant as he got out one of the blue patches and pressed it to the pulse point at her neck.

Cassie felt an immediate surge of energy flowing into her body. It was like the warmth of the healing compress—magnified a thousand times. She smiled. Along with the rush of well-being came a conviction that she could do anything she wanted. "Wow! That's powerful stuff, all right." She flexed her arm and started to reach for the boat to drag it down to the water's edge.

Thorn reacted instantly. "Do not."

"I can do it."

"I know. But you should not." He looked worried. "This was a bad idea."

She pursed her lips as she fought to rein in the sense of power that made her feel as if she could leap into the sky and fly above the trees. "You're right. I'd better pace myself. You get the boat into the water."

Thorn was sliding the craft to the shore when a sound from above made them both look toward the sky. As yet, nothing was visible.

"A plane," Cassie informed Thorn.

"The sheriff?" he asked.

"It could be. Or simply someone on a fishing trip." Her gaze flitted to Glen's craft as she calculated the chances of executing a quick getaway before their unwanted company arrived. "We might be able to make a run for it."

"No. If that is the authorities, they are going to be suspicious about why we are fleeing."

Cassie nodded reluctantly. "They could radio for reinforcements. Or have a reception committee waiting in Anchorage. Damn, I didn't picture it coming down this way."

Cassie's mind raced. Blood pumped through her veins. She knew it was the fight or flight response to danger, and she was as inclined to fight as anything else. When she caught the look on Thorn's face, she commanded herself to take a deep breath.

"We'd better find out who it is." Snatching up the rifle, she grabbed Thorn's hand and tugged him toward the shelter of the pines.

"Hurry. We don't want them to spot us," she commanded when he didn't move fast enough to suit her.

He looked uncertain, yet she was the one who knew the rules of her society, and he had no option except to follow her lead.

When they were safely hidden from view, she turned and looked into the sky, shading her eyes. A small plane circled the lake, then came in for a landing near her guide's plane.

Cassie watched tensely, feeling her heartbeat accelerate as the smaller craft taxied toward shore.

All her attention focused on the man who emerged. He was tall with broad shoulders. His hair was dark and a bit shaggy. He wasn't anyone she'd seen in town, nor was he wearing any kind of uniform. When he leapt from a convenient rock to shore, she saw that his expression was intense, as if he were expecting trouble.

He stopped to inspect their boat. Then he pulled his pack off his shoulder and reached for something inside.

Cassie stifled a low exclamation when she saw what he drew out. He was holding the same kind of energy meter she'd used.

A surge of adrenaline flooded through her body, and she felt as if she were plugged into an electric socket, sucking up an extra charge. She sensed danger, yet she was determined to control the situation. "He knows something," she whispered.

"How can you tell?"

"That meter he's holding. It's like the one Victor supplied me with for the assignment."

"Be calm. He will not—"

She cut Thorn off with an angry interjection. The sound must have carried, because the man's head swiveled in their direction. With a frown, he reached for the pack again.

Cassie wasn't about to let him get the drop on them. Thorn made a grab for her arm, but in her present state, she was much too quick. Bolting from the protection of the pines, she charged down the slight incline toward the intruder, the rifle in front of her as if she were a commando making an assault on an enemy position.

She had the advantage of surprise. ''Hold it right there,'' she said in clipped tones as she cocked the weapon. She had the satisfaction of seeing the stunned expression on his face.

''Are you Cassie Devereaux?'' he asked.

She leveled the rifle toward his chest. ''Who wants to know?''

He shifted his weight from one foot to the other, appraising her.

''Hands up,'' she ordered.

Reluctantly he obeyed.

She jerked the gun at him. ''Who are you? What are you doing here?''

''I'm on a fishing trip.''

''The water's back the other way.''

He shrugged.

''Toss me your wallet,'' she ordered.

When he looked reluctant, she moved the gun again. He kept his eyes on her as he reached into his back pocket, pulled out a billfold and lobbed it onto the ground several feet from where he was standing.

Cassie knelt to scoop it up. In the moment when she took her eyes off him, he lunged. She gasped and went over backward as strong hands jerked away the rifle.

''All right—''

He didn't get a chance to finish. Thorn, who must have circled around, leapt from the underbrush in back of the man. Head lowered, he tackled him around the waist and dragged him to the ground.

The gun went flying. Cassie scrambled for the

weapon as the two men rolled across the pine needles, going at each other with desperate energy.

"Stop," she shouted.

But she might as well have saved her breath. They both ignored her and kept fighting. She raised the rifle, but there was no way she could get a clear shot without endangering Thorn.

The newcomer was bigger. But Thorn was as strong, and his technique was unorthodox. Neither one had the advantage.

Then Thorn was on top. When he reared up to land a solid blow, the intruder looked stunned. "You... you're the man from the picture," he gasped.

Chapter Ten

Thorn pulled the punch before landing the blow on his opponent's jaw.

"Who are you?" Cassie growled at the man with his shoulders on the ground.

"Zeke Chambers."

Cassie shrugged. "Yeah?"

Thorn lifted himself off Zeke and moved protectively to Cassie's side, his body tense, his eyes wary.

Zeke got up, his gaze shifting from Thorn to Cassie and back again.

"How are you mixed up in this?" he asked Thorn.

Cassie didn't let him answer. "None of your business," she said gruffly.

Thorn sighed. "I think you had better give me the gun, Cassandra, before you invoke disaster."

His reference to the ancient prophetess brought her up short. She flushed as she silently acknowledged that she was out of control. Every emotion that seized her was magnified a thousandfold so that she couldn't trust her responses to anything. Worse than that, she had done exactly what Thorn had warned against. She'd rushed Zeke Chambers like a one-woman assault team.

"Thanks, buddy," Zeke muttered to Thorn when the weapon was out of her hands.

She gave them both an angry glare.

Thorn put a restraining hand on her shoulder. "This is not Cassie's normal behavior. She was mauled by a bear. I gave her medication. It seems she is having an extreme reaction."

"Mauled?" Zeke looked at the shredded sleeve of her jacket.

"I'm fine," Cassie snapped. "And that's not relevant," she added, wishing she could stop her lips from flapping before her brain caught up with her mouth.

"So you *are* Cassie Devereaux? Sent here by Victor Kirkland? I know from him you were supposed to investigate an anomalous energy source here."

Cassie eyed him appraisingly. Was he a State Department operative? With the FCC? What? "You work for Victor?"

"Not directly. I'm an anthropological linguist from Johns Hopkins. Victor pulled some strings to get me attached to the international team excavating an ancient site in Greece."

Startled by this new revelation, Cassie looked at Thorn. His expression was grim.

"I'm willing to *exchange* information," Zeke said.

She sighed. "Okay, I *am* Cassie Devereaux."

"So you're here on official business." Zeke turned from her to the saner of the two people he'd just encountered. "How did your picture get into a cave that's been sealed up since the archaic period?"

"What picture?" Cassie demanded.

"Look, I'm tired of being jerked around—by you and Victor."

Cassie took a deep breath, telling herself firmly that her belligerent behavior wasn't doing Thorn any good. "I'm sorry. I got trapped in this situation, too. In fact, we all did. So I'm trying to adjust my thinking."

"Yeah. It looks like Victor didn't want us to get together and exchange information," Zeke said. "Let me show you some very interesting photographs I took at our work site. I'm not going for a gun," he added as a precaution when he reached inside his jacket and brought out an envelope.

"We were excavating a cavern that had been sealed by an enormous rock. On first inspection, the site looked like a nobleman's tomb. But I think that was only a ruse, to hide the inner chamber."

Thorn took the envelope from the newcomer. With great control, he succeeded in keeping his hand from trembling as he slid out the flat rectangles. The pictures—photographs Zeke had called them—were two-dimensional and in black-and-white. Yet even with the crude medium, Thorn felt a frisson go down his spine. The first two photographs showed the excavation site. Next was a picture of an inlaid box, followed by a vase and several pitchers—all products of the native culture he'd known. Like his body, they showed very little sign of their antiquity.

"The household objects came from the tomb," Zeke's measured tones broke into his speculations. "The box with the tablets and the stone carvings were hidden behind a curtain wall at the back."

Thorn passed the photographs to Cassie. "Have you seen anything like these?" he asked, his voice gritty.

"In a museum. They've got some pieces in the

Walters Art Gallery in Baltimore, but not in such excellent shape.''

He nodded and went on to the next photograph. When he realized it showed a page of writing in his own language, the breath froze in his lungs. The letters were tiny, but he could make out the text. It appeared to be a document addressed to future generations, explaining that his people had come from another star system to visit this planet.

''You read this?'' he asked the linguist.

''The writing is similar to ancient Greek, but not identical,'' Zeke said. ''It was during the archaic period that the Greeks switched from picture writing to an alphabet—which led to a tremendous stride forward for their civilization.'' He tapped one of the pictures. ''I haven't had much time to study the inscriptions. But I've made some assumptions.''

Thorn nodded, interested in the man's analysis. But safety demanded keeping his own council. When he thumbed to the next picture, his heart lurched.

The photograph showed an inscription chiseled into stone. Beside it was an illustration—of a naked man imprisoned in a transparent cylinder. What reason could Lodar have for doing this?

''Now you see why I was so startled when I saw your face,'' Zeke commented. ''The guy looks a lot like you.''

Thorn felt his skin prickle. The carving was crude. Still the man looked startlingly like the representation Cassie had drawn of him, with the same slanting eyes and wide mouth. It was enough to convey the impression of his face.

He was almost too stunned to read the text. Somehow he pulled his gaze away from the incriminating picture and read the carved lines. The message wasn't from Lodar, he realized with a jolt. It was from Darnot—the other member of the expedition who'd come to his room that night and kidnapped him.

A harsh laugh escaped Thorn's lips. Darnot's gesture hadn't done the captive much good. It looked as if it was only going to complicate his situation. Was the cave where this information had been hidden the same place where Lodar had left the vaccine he needed to take? Was the vaccine still there? Or was it among the stolen artifacts?

"So how do you figure into this?" Zeke interrupted his churning thoughts. "Are you the umpty-ump-great-great-grandson of the guy who's mentioned in the text? Are you guarding some ancient treasure?"

Thorn was still too stunned to answer.

"That's a good enough explanation," Cassie retorted. She raised her eyes to Zeke. "Did Victor send you here to check up on me?"

"No. I came back to Washington to demand some answers, and he warned me not to interfere."

"But you came, anyway!" she retorted.

"Try to see this from my point of view. First our work site was bombed. Then someone stole the original tablets. All I have left is the pictures."

"*Klat!*" Thorn spat out.

Cassie's gaze shot to him.

"Someone else might be working on the same translations," he suggested. "Did you find us here by following the coordinates?"

"What coordinates?"

At least the man hadn't been able to read the numbers. But given time...

"*Klat,*" Zeke said experimentally, rolling the harsh

syllable around on his tongue. "That's obviously a rather strong expletive. What language is it?"

"Olympian."

Cassie glared at him. Then her expression softened. "The stolen artifacts are extremely valuable. That could be the motive for the threat—not translating the writing."

"Maybe," he conceded. "But we'd better not count on it." Turning, he trotted back to the trees where he and Cassie had left the supplies. For a wild moment he pictured himself simply taking off into the vast wilderness. Instead he stopped and began looking for something in his pack.

Cassie came after him. "Are you all right?"

He didn't answer.

"Tell me what you're thinking," she persisted.

"This man, Zeke Chambers, cannot read the tablets. But I can."

"They're in your language?"

"Yes. The text is a communication left by Lodar's accomplice. It seems he was sorry about the kidnapping. Unfortunately, the text explains exactly where to find me. So if whoever stole the original tablets is interested in information rather than selling stolen antiquities, he may be on his way here."

Cassie sucked in a sharp breath. Involuntarily, she looked up, scanning the sky.

Thorn stifled the same impulse. Instead, he pulled a sensing device out of the pack and began issuing rapid instructions, calling for a long- and short-range scan.

"What are you doing?"

"Setting up an alarm, so we will not be surprised by any more unexpected visitors."

Zeke came over, watching him with interest. "What kind of equipment is that?"

"Classified," Cassie retorted.

"Look, I've been pretty forthcoming with you. Stop turning every question I ask into a dead end," he snapped.

She raised her head and gave him a direct look. "I'm sorry. I know the medication I took is making me act like a Valkyrie on speed. But there's a lot at stake."

"I may be able to help."

"If you're telling the truth."

Zeke's exasperated oath was punctuated by a beep from the sensing device.

Even though Thorn had taken the precaution of getting out the warning mechanism, he was startled by its rapid shift to operational status.

"What was that?" Cassie asked.

"The long-range sensor." Thorn opened a compartment and detached the earpiece. Placing it in his right ear, he listened intently while he manipulated several controls. "We are being scanned for communications on all bands. Since we are not broadcasting, they have not found anything. But they are coming closer. In another airplane, I surmise."

Cassie whirled toward the lake. "We've got to leave."

"Who's coming?" Zeke demanded.

She glared at him. "You probably have a better idea than we do," she said. "One of your esteemed colleagues is leaking information to a third party. Or they pulled off the robbery themselves. Either you innocently led them here, or you're in on the deal."

Zeke cursed. "I'm not feeding you a line. And if someone followed me, I'm sorry."

Thorn nodded tightly. "We do not have much time."

Cassie looked toward Zeke. "Well, you've got a chance to prove you're on the level."

"How?"

"Suppose we take off in separate planes so they won't know which of us to follow. If you can lead them away from me and Thorn, we've got a better chance."

"So you can fly off into the sunset, and I never find you again."

"I guess you have to trust *us,*" Cassie said. "You say you're at Hopkins. We'll get back to you when it's safe."

"Sure."

Thorn watched the two of them. Neither was comfortable with taking all the risk. But there wasn't much time to negotiate.

"Suppose you could be in on breaking a very important anthropological discovery?" Thorn asked.

"Like what?" Zeke countered.

"Like the answers to some perplexing questions about the ancient Greeks. And the key to deciphering the writing in those photographs."

The linguist couldn't keep the excitement out of his eyes.

Cassie gave Thorn a quick look. When he nodded slightly, she reinforced the offer. "Thorn's got the background to give you some answers. And he's not exactly pleased with Victor's meddling in this business, which is why we're being so careful. However, he's agreed to cooperate with a group of my colleagues in Baltimore.''

Zeke sighed. ''I know you're not giving me the whole story. And I'm probably a fool to trust you. But I owe you one.''

''Then let us make haste,'' Thorn suggested.

He and Cassie picked up their equipment, and they all returned to the lake. As they paddled out to the planes, Thorn kept glancing at the sensor, gauging the range of the other approaching craft.

When they drew alongside Cassie's plane, she reached for a dangling rope and maneuvered beside the pontoon. Scrambling out, she opened the door. From his vantage point, the flying machine seemed flimsy and primitive, with what looked like rounded pins holding the metal skin together. Inside, Thorn had to duck low to avoid hitting his head. There were two seats in the front and a long empty area in the rear. Cassie secured the portable boat. When they climbed into what she called the cockpit, he looked at the controls in disbelief.

''Are they coming?'' she asked in response to his indrawn breath.

''Not yet.''

Keeping her attention on the instruments, she began to check various systems. ''I'd like to have more time for this.''

The engines started and the throb vibrated through the whole machine. Then two mechanisms on the wings—propellers, she informed him—began to spin.

He stared at the whirling blades, feeling cold all over.

Cassie spared him a quick glance. ''You look white as a flounder fillet. Are you feeling okay?''

"You fly this machine manually? Continually making decisions about altitude and direction while you are in the air?"

"What did you expect?"

"Analyzer control. Or analyzer assistance, at the very least."

"Yeah, well, there are a few commercial aircraft that fly by wire—as it's called. They don't have such a hot crash record."

"And these?"

"It's safer than driving in a car."

"Why do I not find that comforting?" He gestured toward the banks of dials and gauges. "One person can monitor all that?"

"Yes," she snapped.

Since he'd given her the stimulant, he'd come to mistrust her forceful tone. She was naturally more aggressive than the women of his culture. Half a dose of the medication would have been plenty. "Are you feeling more in control of your reactions?"

"Stop worrying."

He repressed a snappy rejoinder. Probably, he wouldn't get the idiom correct, anyway. Besides, at the moment, he was more worried about their transportation than about Cassie.

Zeke's plane—which had only one engine, he noted—was already skimming along the surface of the lake. As he sat rigid, watching, it rose, gliding into the air like a waterfowl taking flight. After clearing the trees near shore, it banked in a circle around them.

"Fasten your seatbelt," Cassie told Thorn. When he fumbled for the unfamiliar device, she showed him the shoulder strap. "The cabin staff will be coming around with a complimentary beverage of your choice as soon as we reach our cruising altitude,'' she finished with a smirk in her voice.

''What?''

''Never mind.'' She laughed—but her glee was cut short by the sensor. It was emitting a loud beep.

''What was that?'' she asked.

''They will have us in visual range soon,'' Thorn said evenly.

''Not if I can help it.'' Cassie revved the engines and gripped the steering apparatus. The plane began to move, and he superstitiously clamped his fingers over the edge of the seat. They skimmed along the surface of the lake, picked up speed and took flight with surprising ease.

Thorn didn't expel the breath he was holding until the little plane cleared a line of slender pines at the water's edge. Seconds later, a steep hillside covered with green foliage loomed in front of them. Cassie turned in a tight half circle, avoiding the immediate obstacle and aiming for the gap between two mountains.

Thorn felt his ears pop as they climbed. A strong air current made the craft bounce, and he was glad he hadn't eaten recently. Thin ribbons of cloud kept obscuring his vision. Every time they came out of one, he expected to see a cliff straight ahead.

''Can you not gain more altitude?'' he shouted above the roar of the engine as the plane continued weaving around and through the ever-changing contours of the mountains and valleys.

''For our purposes, this is safer.''

He muttered a low reply.

The sensor perched on his knees jiggled and

swayed, but the vibrations didn't interfere with its operation. The beeps were getting closer together—almost continuous.

Glancing over his shoulder, he could see another craft. "Behind us."

"Yeah. Let's hope they decide to follow Zeke." Cassie aimed the plane for the gap between two tall, spiky crags. They plowed through a ribbon of cloud and came out dangerously close to a vertical wall of gray rock.

Cassie made a sharp turn. To Thorn it looked as if she'd narrowly avoided breaking off the left wing. He murmured a low prayer, wishing he had the skills to take control of the craft.

"Not to worry."

"If you say so." He looked behind them and cursed as he saw the other pilot had made his choice. "I am afraid they are not following Zeke Chambers."

"Damn."

Cassie dipped lower to the ground and wove around a cliff. Then she had to pull the nose up sharply again as the terrain rose in front of them. Below he could see the shadow of the aircraft moving across the ground and several white animal shapes bolting for safety.

However, none of Cassie's heart-stopping maneuvers had the desired effect. The pursuers gained on them, coming up dangerously behind their craft. In the next second, he heard a clattering sound above the engine noise. Then a ping against the metal skin of the plane.

"Oh, Lord," Cassie gasped. "They're shooting at us!"

Chapter Eleven

"That was a warning." Outside the plane a harsh male voice boomed over a loudspeaker. "We can easily shoot you down. Land your craft on the nearest lake and surrender. You will not be harmed."

"Like hell." In the small cabin, Cassie's rejoinder was almost as loud as the order from outside. Teeth clenched, she steered the plane into a steep curve that sent them careering through a narrow, twisting valley. Trees sped by so close on either side that Thorn could see the nests of large birds.

Relentlessly, the other plane kept pace.

"The pilot's good," Cassie muttered.

Ahead another band of clouds loomed. Cassie plunged in, broke through, then climbed for more altitude, leaving the valley behind. But not the other pursuing craft.

"They want me, not you," Thorn said. "There is a lake to our right. If you land the craft, I will insist they let you go."

She risked a quick glance in his direction. "You'd be a fool to trust someone who took a shot at you," she countered, her eyes fierce.

He set his teeth, wishing he'd never been persuaded to give her the stimulant.

As they sped onward, she tried various maneuvers with the plane. None of them had any effect. But he knew she was going to keep this up until she shook off their followers or crashed into a mountain.

"There is more mist over there." He pointed toward a large cloud formation off to their right. "Perhaps you could lose them if we stay inside."

"Too dangerous. I don't have radar. So I'm flying blind when I can't see the ground.

Thorn felt his skin crawl. "If you cannot see where you are going, why did you fly into it?"

"It's a calculated risk. Based on my memory of the terrain. I only do it with small clouds."

He swore under his breath. "Do the people with the machine gun have this radar?"

"Probably not."

"Then I have an idea." He began rapidly changing the setting on the sensor. "I've recalibrated the machine to tell what obstructions are ahead."

Cassie nodded tightly, never taking her concentration from the task of flying the small craft through the mountain valleys.

Thorn stared at the sensor screen, trying to orient himself to the display, wishing fervently that he had more time to practice the required technique.

But time was in short supply. Behind them, another clatter sound erupted. It was followed by a ping as a small hole opened in the floor of the plane near his left boot.

Thorn's foot danced away, and Cassie looked down. "Damn. That's too close for comfort."

"Land or be shot down," the voice on the speaker

boomed. This time the sound was so loud it rattled his eardrums.

Cassie spat out an answering expletive as she dipped the wing and plunged the plane to the right. A tall spike of gray rock whizzed past a few feet from his window.

Ahead was the white bank of cloud.

"Can you guide me in and out?" she asked urgently.

Eyes narrowed, he stared at the screen, making sure he understood the readings for distances and the speed of the plane. "Yes."

Cassie steered toward the obscuring white. Seconds later the cloud pressed in around them, wiping everything from view. Mountains, valleys, rock and sky disappeared as if they'd never existed.

Thorn swallowed hard. Eyes narrowed, he stared at the instrumentation. Navigating through this was harder than he'd thought. The readings changed abruptly. "Dead ahead. Climb," he ordered.

Cassie obeyed instantly. They shot out of the mist and over the top of a peak. Seconds later, a bone-jarring explosion sounded behind them, and their fragile plane shook from the impact of the shock waves.

He shuddered. "They hit the mountain."

"I think they got what they deserved." Cassie circled back. Looking down, Thorn saw the crumpled aircraft. Seconds later, it burst into flames.

Cassie grimaced and reached for a piece of equipment Thorn hadn't seen her use before. When she began to speak, he realized it was a communications unit. "This is TX278JP calling Anchorage. I want to report a downed plane." When she finished the conversation, she looked at the hole by his foot. "Let's hope the excitement helps take their attention away from us. If we're lucky, nobody will notice the bullet holes in this baby until we're back on the east coast. Or maybe they'll assume it's from an old scrape Glen got himself into."

"STOP THE CAR."

"What's wrong? You see something in the woods?" Cassie had felt more comfortable since they'd arrived back in Maryland, but she wasn't about to let her guard down. Her foot bounced from the accelerator to the brake of the rented Blazer she was steering up the long driveway of Katie and Mac McQuade's Howard County home. Leaning toward the windshield, she peered at the sun-dappled shade under the tall oaks and maples.

"Sorry. I want to talk to you before we confront the others," Thorn said.

The narrow road had no shoulder. So she pulled to the side of the blacktop and shifted into park. Hoping she was masking her inner tension, she gave Thorn a reassuring smile. "Everything's going to be all right."

"I doubt it."

She found his hand and stroked her fingers over his, the physical contact comforting as always. "We're safe here. I don't mean just at Mac and Katie's. I mean, this is my home territory. You can trust my friends. We've been through a lot together. These people organized my sister Marissa's escape from San Marcos. They have connections and talents that can help you."

"You are putting yourself in too much trouble for me," he said in a grating voice. "I do not like it."

"Thorn, I know the way the world works."

He sighed. "Yes, I have had ample demonstrations of your skills at manipulating people and making illegal arrangements over the past few days. Without you, I would probably be in a jail cell in Anchorage or detained by the military."

She didn't bother to deny the observation. When they'd landed at a town called Wasila, she'd done a verbal tap dance for the airport authorities. Then, instead of checking into a hotel, she'd paid cash on the rental of a fishing shack while she arranged private transportation to Baltimore.

Thorn sighed. "I understand why you hired a bush pilot to fly us to Vancouver. I understand why we have stayed in two different hotels instead of your house. I know why you have been making phone calls since we arrived in Baltimore. But I do not understand why you are endangering a whole gathering of people because of me."

"My friends are a very supportive group. We all rally around when one of us is in trouble."

"You are not in trouble. I am."

Her grip tightened on his hand, and the words she'd been longing to say tumbled from her lips. "Thorn, I love you. That makes your problems mine."

He cursed softly under his breath. "I was afraid you would say something like that."

She gave a strained laugh around the lump that threatened to block her windpipe. "Well, now I know where I stand."

"I do not think so." He pulled her across the seat. Drawing her against his chest, he wrapped his arms around her so tightly that she gasped for breath. After several heartbeats, he began to speak in a gritty voice. "Cassie, I could have said those words to you the first night we made love. I did not want to burden you with entanglements. I did not want you feeling obligated to me. I still do not."

Her eyes misted as she raised her head and looked into his face. "You felt that way, too?" she breathed.

"Yes. But the knowledge can only be a hardship for you."

"No—"

"My future is uncertain. And being close to me could be deadly."

"I'm willing to take the risk. That's my decision."

"Do you think the incident with the airplane and the assault weapon was a random act of violence?"

"Congratulations, you get an *A* for twentieth century philosophy. But I don't agree with your conclusions. They may have been shooting at us, but I don't believe they wanted to kill you. They wanted us to set down so they could capture you."

"To dissect me? Or pump me for the secrets of the universe, do you think?"

Cassie shuddered as goose bumps swept across her skin. Since they'd left the bunker under the mountain, she'd become more and more aware that they were playing a game with sky-high stakes. Her only salvation was to believe she and Thorn were going to win.

"Whatever they want, I'm going to make sure they don't get their hands on you. So I'm afraid you're stuck with me—at least until we figure out who sent the plane, and why."

"Stuck is hardly the term I would use."

"What, then?"

He lowered his head and took her mouth in a kiss that started out almost savagely and banked to something approaching raging passion. Her hands ranged over his shoulders and threaded through his hair. His hands moved to cup her breasts, kneading and stroking, and finding the hardened tips with his thumbs, making her moan into his mouth.

When he finally lifted his lips from hers, they both drew shuddering breaths. She pressed her forehead against his shoulder, trying to convince herself that making love in a car in her friends' driveway would be risky. She looked at Thorn apologetically. "We'd better not."

"I will defer to your judgement again," he said in a rough voice.

"Sometimes I hate being right."

The honk of a car horn made them both jump and swivel around.

Marissa and Jed had drifted up behind them in the driveway and were grinning like Cheshire cats.

Cassie slammed the Blazer into gear, and the car groaned forward. Then she remembered to release the emergency brake.

When they reached the parking area, Marissa hopped out of her own car, trotted over and folded her into a close hug. "I let you out of my sight for a couple of days, and you get yourself into deep kimchi," she whispered.

"I'm afraid so."

They both turned to see Marissa's husband, Jed Prentiss, and Thorn shaking hands. Cassie repressed a little smile. Thorn had learned the greeting from watching television. To look at him, you wouldn't know it had been totally unfamiliar a few days ago.

In fact, to look at him, you wouldn't know he was an astronaut who had stepped from a delta cylinder less than a week ago. Granted, his coloring was a little unusual. Yet dressed in jeans and a button-down shirt, he could have fit in with the crowd at Owings Mills Mall food court just fine. Cassie had longed to show him some of the fun aspects of modern civilization. But she hadn't been willing to take a chance on the mall or a movie theater or a gourmet restaurant, in case whoever had sent the plane to Alaska was looking for her. So she and Thorn had been hiding out in Towson and had taken only one quick shopping trip.

Marissa drew her sister aside. "I guess I'm not the only Devereaux sister who's found her soul mate," she whispered. "He's gorgeous. And since you've given your heart to him, I know he's got all those qualities we were looking for but thought we could never find." She shot her husband a quick glance, then turned back to Cassie.

Cassie gave her a tremulous smile. "Yes, he's wonderful. And we can live a long happy life together—after we work out a few major problems."

Marissa squeezed her shoulder. "You can count on us to help."

"I know. But things are kind of complicated."

"They were when Jed came down to San Marcos to rescue me," Marissa reminded her.

"When you hear about Thorn, you'll know we've got some special problems," Cassie whispered.

The private conversation was cut off as they reached the porch of the McQuades' redwood-and-stone rancher.

Katie came out and gave Cassie a hug. Inside, the rest of the invited guests were trying not to stare at the new arrivals.

Taking a deep breath, Cassie stepped across the threshold. She trusted these people with her life. And she'd made the same commitment for Thorn. Now she couldn't suppress a little twinge of doubt. If someone made even the smallest slip, it would mean disaster.

Inside, Katie and some of the other women had set up a lunch buffet purchased from a gourmet shop in Columbia. Anybody who stumbled in might think they were having a Saturday afternoon party, Cassie mused. Except that all conversation had suddenly stopped.

Cassie plastered a smile onto her face. "Hi. I'd like you all to meet Thorn," she said, with a little nod to Zeke Chambers, who had already had the pleasure. Zeke was standing to one side, trying to look calm as he glanced from her to Thorn.

Zeke was with Elizabeth Egan, one of his graduate students who also worked part-time for Erin Stone. She did highly confidential work helping adoptees locate their birth parents, and Erin had vouched for her. In turn, Elizabeth had reassured Cassie about Zeke's integrity. But there had really been no question about leaving him out of the meeting. He already knew too much. And if he were left to his own devices, he could be dangerous. Better to include him in her circle of confidants.

Zeke and Thorn were staring at each other as if a silent message were passing between them.

"You never did tell me your profession," Zeke said.

"I am an exolinguist."

"Ah. Then I guess we have a lot to talk about."

"Yes. I am sorry I was not very forthcoming earlier," Thorn apologized.

"I can understand why."

Cassie saw Katie listening, which precluded any possibility of drawing Thorn aside and asking about the undercurrent running below the conversation with Zeke.

But the odd exchange increased her feeling of disquiet as she went through the motions of making introductions. Erin and Travis Stone, Abby Franklin and Steve Claiborne, Sabrina Barkley and Dan Cassidy. Katie and Mac McQuade, and Cam Randolph and Jason Zacharias, there without their wives.

There was considerable interest in Thorn—generated by the few guarded things she'd said. They knew he was in hiding, that he hadn't done anything illegal and that he had information that could be important. She could feel questions simmering below the calm surface of the introductions. But she also knew her friends would let her do things her way.

Cassie felt a nervous smile on her face as everyone found chairs. She was usually pretty articulate, but when she'd been trying to think of what to say, the words kept turning to mush in her head.

She'd learned the startling truth of Thorn's unique circumstances in slow steps. The Light Street Irregulars, as they'd begun to call themselves, were about to hear a science-fiction story in compressed form, and she couldn't be sure how they would react.

They were all waiting. She cleared her throat.

"When Marci was in trouble in San Marcos," she began, "you heard a pretty incredible tale from Jed about how she'd been kidnapped and was being held incommunicado." There were murmurs and nods around the room. "Well, something similar happened to Thorn. Only it's a lot worse, if you can believe that." She shot her sister an apologetic look.

"Marci was scooped up by General Sanchez because she was caught raiding his secret files. Thorn's only crime was speaking up for the, uh, native people he met when he came here. He was kidnapped and... imprisoned for a long time, and he can't be rescued by his own people. And he has to stay in hiding, because someone's trying to capture him." She gulped. "Maybe kill him."

The faces around the room were sympathetic. Yet she hadn't gotten to the hard part.

When she started to take up the narrative, Thorn clamped his fingers over hers. "Let me speak for myself. I do not like coming to these people as a supplicant."

She wanted to argue that she was better prepared, yet she had to respect his wishes.

"I told Cassie that when she heard my story, she might think I was lying. Or suffering from delusions. So I have been thinking of how I might make myself credible to a group of strangers." He reached into the carry pack he'd brought and took out a little box, which he held in his lap. The sense of anticipation in the room was palpable.

"Do you still have those photographs from the archaeological dig?" he asked Zeke.

The linguist handed them over.

Thorn thumbed through the black-and-white photos, selected several, including the vase and the box, and passed them around the circle. "These are pictures of artifacts discovered at a site in Greece that was sealed for almost three thousand years. The objects were stolen, but I believe I can show you more lifelike representations, as well as some other images that will be of interest.''

Cassie felt a little shiver go up her spine as she waited to see what Thorn was going to do. From the expression on his face, she knew that he was getting a certain amount of satisfaction out of creating suspense.

When Katie handed the photos back to him, he opened the side of the box, inserted the pictures and snapped the door shut. Then he began to work some controls.

There was a collective gasp as a picture of the vase appeared in the center of the room. No. Not a picture, exactly. A three-dimensional color image that looked as solid as the real thing. Only it was hanging in midair three feet from the floor. Thorn touched a control, slowly rotating the object. Another adjustment enlarged the size by about one-third.

Zeke sprang from his seat and bent toward the artifact. ''That's the vase I took out of the cave, all right. The one that was stolen, along with the rest of the valuables.'' Cautiously he reached to touch it. His hand passed through the image, and his fingers closed around empty air.

''How did you do that?'' Cam Randolph asked.

''A sophisticated projection system.''

Zeke clasped his hands behind his back as he examined the detailed scenes on the sides of the vase. ''It shows men and women coming to a temple to worship a god.'' He flicked a quick gaze at Thorn and then back at the vase.

"Not a god," Thorn said in a gritty voice. "A man named Lodar who enjoyed wielding power. A man who pretended to work miracles—by using equipment that people did not understand. Like this device." He gestured toward the box resting on his knees.

An excited buzz of conversation broke out around the room.

Thorn cut off the chatter by making the vase disappear. Almost immediately, he replaced it with one of the stone tablets. The one showing the man imprisoned in the glass cylinder.

Cassie saw everyone looking from the projection to Thorn. They saw the resemblance, all right.

Thorn addressed Zeke. "I inferred from our conversation a few minutes ago that you have made some progress with this text." He pointed toward the lines of symbols.

"As a matter of fact, I did. Do you want me to keep it between us?"

"No. I think it is best for the group to hear what you discovered."

Cassie felt as if a bolt of electricity had shot through her body. All at once, she realized how cleverly Thorn was handling this. He wasn't going to try to prove he was from another planet and that he'd been in suspended animation for almost three thousand years. By itself, the information was the stuff of science fiction. It would go down a lot more smoothly if it came from Zeke Chambers's observations.

She tuned in on Zeke's voice as he said, "There are some differences in the consonants between Olympian and Greek. But once you know what to look for, you can make some pretty good guesses based on ancient Greek vocabulary." He nodded toward Thorn. "I'm sure you can help me with the words that are giving me problems."

"Certainly. But I am interested in what you have discovered on your own."

Zeke gave him a little smile.

"Why do you call it Olympian?" Elizabeth Egan questioned.

"After the point of origin."

"You mean Mount Olympus? The mythical place where the Greek gods were supposed to dwell?" Abby clarified.

"No. Another planet in a solar system about thirty light-years from here," Zeke told her.

"What?" Elizabeth's exclamation was echoed around the room.

"The text I've translated is about a group of extraterrestrial astronauts who visited ancient Greece."

"You're joking, aren't you?" Travis Stone asked. He shot a glance at Cassie. "We're not here to investigate an ancient astronauts hoax, are we?"

"No," she snapped.

"Let's look at the fraud theory," Zeke suggested. "Any deception would have to be of *ancient* origin because the text has been sealed up for almost three thousand years."

"You're sure of that?" Steve Claiborne probed.

"An archaeological team moved a boulder at the entrance to the site two months ago. Last week, an explosion cleared away the barrier to the inner room where the artifacts and tablets were found. If I still had them, I could prove their age by carbon dating."

Steve nodded.

"Last night I was finally able to decipher some numbers included with the text and the picture of the man in the cylinder,'' Zeke continued. ''They turned out to be geographic coordinates pinpointing the Alaskan location where Cassie was sent by the FCC to investigate anomalous energy readings.''

''The cave in Greece is connected with the site in Alaska?'' Elizabeth clarified.

Zeke nodded. ''They both have the same energy signature. That's how I found Cassie and Thorn.''

Cassie felt light-headed. She could sense everyone waiting to see exactly how all this was related to Thorn. And she wanted to shout out the truth. But that would undermine the credibility of Zeke's logical explanation. So she clamped her lips together and forced herself to stay silent.

''Now that I can read the coordinates on the tablets, I know they indicate where the space expedition's exolinguist—'' he paused and glanced at Thorn ''—was left in suspended animation after he had a policy dispute with the expedition leader.''

''Are you sure you've translated correctly?'' Steve demanded.

''Yes. I've been working on this thing twenty hours a day since I got back from Alaska.''

The room erupted in a spontaneous, excited buzz.

''Okay, I want to make sure I'm following this right,'' Dan Cassidy persisted, his gaze swinging from Zeke to Thorn and back again. ''It sounds like you're asking us to swallow the story that our mysterious visitor was a member of that extraterrestrial expedition. That he's the man who was put in suspended animation.''

Debate swirled around her, until Cassie couldn't

take it anymore. Rising to her feet, she looked around at her friends. When she spoke, her voice cut through the hum of voices like a knife slicing through flesh. "If you argue about it long enough, he'll be dead."

Chapter Twelve

Thorn reached for Cassie's hand and tugged. The starch went out of her legs, and she sank heavily into her seat.

"What do you mean—he'll be dead?" Dan demanded.

Cassie swallowed around the lump blocking her windpipe. She hadn't intended to blurt anything about Thorn's health. She'd simply been too strung out to keep herself under control.

Katie came over and knelt beside her. "Is Thorn sick?" she asked gently. "Something contagious?"

"Not to you," Cassie retorted.

"The members of our first expedition reacted unfavorably to some of the bacteria on your planet," Thorn elaborated. "Our healers produced a vaccine. I was due for a booster. The team leader left some of it for me. I presume it would be in the cave Zeke's team discovered."

Zeke made a low sound that sent a shiver down Cassie's spine. "If it was in the cave, it's not there now," he said tightly. "Everything was stolen."

"You found concealed storage chambers?" Thorn asked urgently.

"Yes. That's how we got the box and the tablets."

Cassie's vision blurred. She struggled to stay on top of her emotions, but it took a monumental effort. She'd been afraid of this.

"We should test your immune system as soon as possible," Katie said to Thorn, then glanced at her husband, Mac.

"We can go from here to the lab," he agreed.

"Thank you," Cassie whispered, afraid that if she raised her voice she'd start to cry. Then she reached for anger to push away her dread. Turning to Dan, she demanded, "Is that all right? Or should we turn Thorn in to the Maryland State Board of Health as a public safety hazard? Or what about the Pentagon? They'd love to have him."

Thorn grabbed her hand again. "Cassie, you and Zeke are familiar with my very strange history. Everybody else is hearing it for the first time. Perhaps—what do you call it? DNA testing would prove that I am the genuine article."

"We'd have to wait several weeks for the results," Katie told him, but she looked excited at the prospect of doing the procedure.

Trying to keep her voice steady, Cassie addressed the group. "Let me give you a little more background." In staccato bursts she told them about the avalanche. About her reaction to the strange underground station and the naked man she'd found in the delta cylinder. She related most of the saga—up to and through the attack by the other plane and her return to Baltimore. She left out only a few very personal details. But she suspected that her women friends and her sister were reading between the lines, that they knew very well why she was so committed to Thorn.

When she finished, Marissa swiped the back of her hand at the corners of her eyes.

"I'd like to get a look at this installation," Jason said.

"Opening it up is too dangerous for Thorn right now," Cassie responded. "We don't know who's after him and why... Whether they want to use him or eliminate him." She shivered.

Jed slung his arm over Marissa's shoulder. "A couple of months ago, I thought I'd found out how much trouble one of the Devereaux sisters could get herself into. Cassie, you top my wife."

"Are you saying you believe me and Thorn?" Cassie asked.

He laughed. "Your story is so crazy, it has to be true."

Cassie let out a long sigh. "Thank you."

One by one, the rest of the group joined in the endorsement. Cassie slid a sidewise glance at Thorn. He looked a bit dazed, as if he couldn't believe the vote of confidence. Silently she leaned her back against his chest and he put his arm around her.

"If you can't keep Thorn's secret absolutely confidential, he's in grave danger," she warned. When everyone agreed, she felt her anxiety creep down another notch.

"Well, I think I know who was behind the aircraft attack," Zeke said. "I've been doing some research, and I'm putting my money on Jacques Montague, the man who financed the Greek dig."

"Doesn't he live on an island fortress in the Mediterranean?" Jason asked. "Not far from Sicily."

Zeke looked surprised. "You've heard of him?

"I make a hobby of keeping tabs on power-mad nuts. He's a very unconventional character—from what I've learned. Rich enough to have his own island and almost anything else money can buy."

"Yeah," Zeke broke in. "He inherited family wealth and parlayed that into billions. He's had a team of linguists working for the past ten years, trying to translate Linear A."

"What's that?" Jason asked.

Elizabeth answered. "A very early Greek written language. Nobody's been able to crack it."

"But Montague's apparently determined," Zeke added.

"Why?" Cassie asked.

"He's interested in antiquities and ancient burial sites. And the mythology of various cultures," Zeke answered.

"If he stole the tablets, then his team could have been ahead of you on the translations," Cassie said to Zeke. When she glanced at Thorn, she realized he must have been thinking the same thing.

"Maybe he thinks Thorn's technology can expand his power base," Jason suggested.

"He's rich enough and arrogant enough to try it," Zeke agreed.

"I am not interested in helping him," Thorn remarked.

"Montague doesn't know that yet," Jason said. "And he's accustomed to forcing solutions out of people."

"Well, we have the resources to discover his points of vulnerability and go on the offensive," Jason said. "If we have to, we can work up something like the witness protection program for Thorn. A new identity so he won't have to keep looking over his shoulder."

Cassie felt a little dazed by the outpouring of goodwill and concrete suggestions.

"How else can we help you?" Abby Franklin asked.

"We need a place to hide out until the Montague threat is neutralized," Cassie said. "When we know Thorn is safe, we can make plans for the future."

"How about our vacation house on the Choptank River?" Travis Stone asked.

"I'll beef up the security system," Cam Randolph added.

"Thank you," Cassie breathed.

Still looking a bit overwhelmed, Thorn added his thanks.

"So now that we know we've got a real live spaceman right here in the McQuade living room, we're itching to ask you some questions," Cam said.

"Of course," Thorn agreed.

"How does our technology compare to yours?"

"We are more advanced in many ways. But you have a number of things that I find very pleasing. Like chocolate. It's wonderful."

"But he's not so sure about our small airplanes," Cassie volunteered. "He couldn't believe something so clunky could fly!"

Thorn flushed slightly. "Let me tell you what I do like. Your world has incredible variety. Take your music. Jazz. Rock. Classical. Rap."

"You like *that?*" Erin asked.

"The rhythms are interesting. Your entertainment media have programs I could never have imagined. Like animated cartoons. My favorite is the 'Simpsons' because of the comments it makes about your society.'' He laughed. ''On a slightly more elevated note, I long to see your great museums. The Louvre. The Prado. The Smithsonian.''

''I hope we have a lot to offer you,'' Abby said.

''I have Cassie to help me. And the rest of you.''

Cassie felt her heart expand as she looked at the circle of eager faces around them. Her friends really were extraordinary.

''If I must stay hidden, I would like to keep busy writing down technological information from my civilization that you might find useful,'' Thorn continued.

''I'll lend you a laptop computer,'' Cam offered. ''And anything else you need.''

''Can you go back home again?'' Erin asked wistfully.

Thorn's expression became grave. ''You have no ship that could make the journey to my sun. Even if I were able to return, everything familiar to me would be long gone. I do not know how far my people have advanced. Or even whether my civilization still exists.''

''That must be hard for you,'' Abby said in a gentle voice.

''I have come to terms with it.''

Still, his words sobered the assembly. Questions were more subdued, and the meeting ended soon after.

When Cassie came back from saying goodbye to her friends, she found Thorn sitting with a preoccupied expression.

''So?'' she asked softly.

He raised his eyes to her, and she saw a look of

wonder. "You said your friends would help me. I hardly dared hope for such a...vote of confidence. Would all of your people demonstrate such vision—such faith in a stranger from another galaxy?"

She didn't need to think about his question. "No. The Light Street Irregulars are special."

ZEKE CHAMBERS STARED wearily at the screen of the high-performance workstation Cam Randolph had installed in the apartment he was temporarily renting. Since he was still officially on leave from Hopkins, he'd elected to stay out of circulation until things could be resolved with Thorn.

When he'd gone chasing off to Alaska, he hadn't realized he was taking on an enormous responsibility. But in the meeting, he'd come to understand that Thorn's freedom—and probably his life—depended on keeping his secret.

For the past week he'd been working eighteen hours a day writing a trumped-up explanation of why the Olympian tablets had to be an extremely clever fake. But he wasn't going to publish the article unless someone came forward with the real material.

The phone buzzed on the desk next to the computer. He glanced at the clock. Half past midnight. Was there trouble out at the Stones' vacation home where Thorn and Cassie were staying?

But it wasn't one of the Light Street group calling. The voice on the other end of the line was Marie Pindel, the team leader from the Greek site.

"Zeke, finally."

He thought about the dozens of messages she'd left on his machine at home. At the dig site, he'd trusted

Marie. But someone had betrayed them, and she was the only other person who knew about the secret find.

"How did you get through?" he finally answered.

"I have my sources. Are you all right?"

"Yeah. Any news on the stolen artifacts?" he asked.

"So far—nothing. And the authorities have fewer leads than on the explosion at the cave. But they don't think the two crimes are connected."

Zeke made a noncommittal reply.

"You've made some progress with the pictures you took?" There was an odd inflection in her voice, curiosity and something more. It was as if she already knew the answer and were waiting to hear what he'd say.

"I've found conclusive evidence that the tablets were a very clever hoax. I can send you my report next week."

Marie sighed. "Are you sure?"

"Positive."

"Then I guess whoever stole the material is going to be very disappointed."

"By the way, Marie, did you mention our discovery to anyone at the site on the day of the robbery?"

"No, of course not." She sounded indignant at the possible accusation.

"To anyone else, then?"

"Only Montague. But he was our sponsor."

Montague! How convenient that she'd passed on that information to the man who was after Thorn. "It's late. I've got to go. I'll send you copies of the material soon." He hung up the phone and immediately dialed Cam Randolph.

CASSIE LAY on her stomach somewhere between bliss and nirvana. A Mozart symphony played softly in the background. The quilt-covered exercise mat under her was firm but silky. And Thorn's strong fingers, lightly coated with scented oil, were finding and massaging pressure points on her shoulders she hadn't known existed.

Taking his time, he moved down her back, along her spine, to her buttocks.

"Ahh." A long satisfied sigh escaped from her lips.

"Let's work on the front."

A tingle of anticipation went through her. She'd learned a lot about Thorn in the past ten days while they'd been hiding out at the Stones' Eastern Shore estate. He had the broadest range of abilities she'd ever seen in one person. He sucked up information like a computer, and he knew how to give pleasure she'd never dreamed possible.

However, as she rolled to her back, the phone on the secure line rang.

"Damn."

He gave her a wry smile and pressed the speaker button. It was Jo O' Malley, Cam's wife. A private detective, she was acting as liaison for the intelligence team.

"How are you doing?" she asked.

Cassie giggled. "Lucky this isn't a picture phone."

Jo laughed. "I hate to interrupt anything important. But I have some information for you."

Cassie's mood instantly sobered as she grabbed a robe from the chair. Thorn didn't bother to get dressed. By now, she was used to his casual nudity.

"Jason stopped by with a report on Montague's stronghold," Jo said.

Cassie waited nervously. They'd been trying for days to figure out how to get a man on the island. So far, it was no go.

"Anything we can use?" Thorn asked.

Jo made a clucking sound. "Well, the guys have given up on the subtle approach. Unfortunately, I don't think we're going to assault his island anytime soon. Jason's sources have found out he's got a two-hundred-man private army. And the grounds are sprinkled with computer-controlled explosive charges. If you step on the wrong patch of ground at the wrong time, you've had it. The full report will come to you by fax this afternoon."

Cassie swallowed hard. Computer-controlled land mines and a private army. But then, the more she learned about Montague, the more repelled she was by the man.

"Listen, I'm sorry I interrupted," Jo said. "Go back to whatever you were doing."

But the mood had been broken. It was hard to think about making love when images of exploding land mines kept flashing in her mind.

"Want to have lunch?" Cassie asked Thorn. "The caterer brought down some more of that cherry cheesecake you like."

"Mmm-hmm," he said with studied casualness.

She turned away, found her shorts and T-shirt and bustled down the hall to the kitchen. In some ways, this enforced vacation at the shore was like an idyllic honeymoon. However, when she least expected it, the shadows swept down like vultures.

This time, a simple discussion about lunch had

made her stomach knot. She'd been working overtime to tempt Thorn with high-calorie dishes—and they both knew why. His metabolism was striving hard to fight off the illness—and using up huge quantities of energy in the process.

As she walked into the kitchen, Cassie superstitiously rapped on the nearest cabinet. So far, Thorn was healthy. In fact, he had more energy and more drive than any other two men.

While Katie and Mac tried to find a cure for his illness, they were using an interim technique that had been developed from AIDS research. Because they'd caught Thorn before he went into a critical phase, they'd been able to use the antibodies present in his own blood to boost his immune system. Still, it wasn't a permanent solution. And she couldn't repress a stab of dread. In the past few days she'd been forced to acknowledge another worry—something she should discuss with Katie. Instead she told herself that it could always wait a little longer. Because if she confirmed her suspicions, then she'd have someone else to be frightened for besides Thorn.

"Want to try something unique this afternoon?"

She arranged her features into a look of anticipation before turning toward the door.

Thorn, who had finally dressed, was grinning. "It was not an indecent proposal."

"A girl can hope."

"I was writing up a report for Cam last night, and it gave me an idea. My people colonized our oceans before we went out into space. So we developed devices for undersea exploration."

"Interesting." She took a carton of Thai cream

curry from the refrigerator, transferred it to a serving dish and set it in the microwave.

Thorn held up what looked like a pair of elongated beads. "These duplicate the functions of a fish's gills and allow a human being to extract oxygen from water."

"That sounds impossible."

"It is a simple principle, really. When I was trying to decide what we might need after we escaped from the cave, I packed two sets. In case we had to submerge before getting to your airplane."

"The water temperature in Alaska would have killed us in a few minutes."

"I know that now. But it is much warmer here." He gestured toward the river. "After lunch we can try it out, if you want."

"We?"

"You. One of us should stand guard."

She nodded tightly. Another casual conversation that had turned into a reminder of their peril.

"Want to eat on the deck?" she asked quickly.

Thorn nodded. Since his confinement, he'd craved being in the fresh air—which made the Stones's house perfect. They could stroll in the gardens or along the sandy beach.

Thorn helped her carry out the meal. The Thai curry and the cheesecake were both a success.

"Eating like this is going to make me fat," Cassie said with a sigh.

"You need a nice brisk swim."

"Give me a few minutes."

After relaxing in the sun for a while, Cassie changed into a modest two-piece bathing suit.

When she reappeared on the deck, Thorn stood and

gave her a wolf whistle, a skill he'd been practicing for the past few days.

Her cheeks heated. "I thought this was a subdued suit."

"I like the way it shows off your breasts."

"Are Olympian men always so direct?"

"When they have not had sex for three thousand years."

She laughed. "You've had plenty in the past couple of weeks. Are all Olympian men so, uh, verily?"

"Am I unusual—for your species?"

"Well, I haven't made a very extensive personal study, you understand. But I suspect from the articles in the women's magazines that you're...remarkable."

His eyes twinkled. "Perhaps we could work up an infomercial. Sex Secrets of the Ancient Gods Revealed. Techniques that will keep you going longer than the Energizer bunny. For only nineteen ninety-five plus ten dollars shipping and handling."

"Throw in a video on your massage techniques, and you can charge an extra fifteen dollars."

"We will run it right after "Quantum Leap" on the sci-fi channel."

Cassie smiled. "You like that show."

"I pick up pointers from Sam. He has to cope with a new identity every time he leaps."

"Well, you're stuck with me for good."

He started to answer. She cut off the words with a kiss. For long moments they feasted on each other, and she felt the erotic energy building between them.

The color of his eyes had deepened. "I love the look on your face when you are aroused," he said huskily.

"Yours, too."

"Honey, if you want those breathing lessons anytime before dinner, we had better get going."

He held her gaze for several more seconds before handing Cassie the beads.

She jiggled the small plugs in her hand. "That's really all I need?"

"They have special filters that remove the oxygen from the water. Once they are in the nose, you simply breath normally."

"This I've got to see."

"Try them now, and get used to the sensation."

Self-consciously, she inserted the cylinders. It felt as if she had wads of cotton in her nose. But when she pressed her mouth shut and sucked in a draft of air, it came through with no trouble. "So far so good."

They strolled down to the edge of the property where Cassie disconnected the sensors that ringed the grounds.

Thorn sighed as they stepped onto the dock. "This is a beautiful place. And I love being alone with you. But there is so much I want to see and do."

"I know. It's hard being forced to stay in one spot. As soon as this is over, I'm going to take you on the best damn tour of this planet any travel agent ever arranged. I'll show you Paris, London, Rome. We'll go to an Orioles game. A live volcano. The Met. Stonehenge. Anywhere you want."

"If we have time."

She felt a stab of fear. "We will."

He gave her a rueful little smile. "I am sorry. I am not following the rules."

"They're your rules." She gave him a critical inspection. "Is something wrong? Are you feeling sick? Is that it?"

"No," he said, much too quickly.

"Thorn?"

"I should learn to live for the moment."

"For the future."

"All right," he agreed, but Cassie knew he was sorry he'd started the discussion.

She wanted to take him by the shoulders, shake him hard and insist that he wasn't going to leave her. Not when they gave each other so much. Instead she turned toward the water while she got control of her features.

"There is a navigation channel cut in the river bottom, so it's pretty deep at the end of the pier," she said in an almost normal voice. "Is it all right to dive with these things in my nose?"

"It is better to submerge more gently—so you do not dislodge the plugs," Thorn answered, striving for the same neutral tone.

They were halfway down the thirty-foot dock when a noise from behind made them both pivot.

Two muscular men had come out from under the pier and were standing on the beach, their lower pant legs and sneakers soaking. Lord, they must have been waiting for her and Thorn to leave the protected compound, she realized with a sick feeling. She'd thought Thorn was safe in this quiet corner of the world; it was only an illusion.

"Run," she shouted.

But there was nowhere to escape. The intruders stood solidly blocking their exit. One had a chest and arms like a boxer. The other had the long legs of a cross-country runner. But the important point was that they were both holding machine guns.

"Hands up," one of the men ordered, pointing the gun toward the center of her chest. The other covered Thorn as he bent toward a portable communications unit from his collar and spoke in a low voice.

Pure, stark terror shot through Cassie as she looked wildly from their captors toward the sparkling water. A motorboat that had been bobbing picturesquely in the sun was now heading at top speed toward the dock. Seconds later, the man at the wheel cut the engine, and two more tough-looking thugs jumped out to join the impromptu party. Only it wasn't impromptu, Cassie realized. Someone had planned this carefully.

"Let's go," one of the newcomers ordered.

"Wait," Thorn protested.

The captor gave him a shove, and he grabbed a post to keep from falling.

Cassie was instantly at his side. "Leave him alone."

"Shut up and get moving."

"You only want me. Let her go, and I will cooperate," Thorn argued.

"Oh, you'll definitely cooperate," the speaker retorted, his voice icy. "One way or the other."

Cassie's heart was pounding so fast that she could hardly breathe. She had seconds to make a decision. Thorn. She had to stay with him. But then no one would know what had happened. If she escaped, she could bring help.

She didn't have to pretend terror as she let herself be led toward the boat. It was now or never. At the last moment, instead of stepping into the craft, she plunged over the end of the dock and dove into the cold water.

Above her she heard a curse. It was followed by a shout and the angry clattering of the machine gun. Bullets sprayed into the water as she frantically dove and kicked for the river bottom.

Chapter Thirteen

Panic fueled Cassie as she clawed her way down into the dark water. Something hot shot past her thigh. A bullet! Too close for comfort.

She pressed her lips together and kept moving, trying to put as much distance as she could between herself and the surface where the machine guns still clattered.

To her intense relief, the noise faded as she lengthened the distance between herself and the pier. But she couldn't stay underwater forever.

Above her, she heard a splash. Lord, had they come in after her? Surely not with a gun, her rational mind chided.

Yet her skin crawled as she anticipated the feel of hard fingers closing around her ankle.

No one caught up with her. Perhaps they couldn't see her in the murky water at the bottom. But she'd have to come up for air. Soon. And the intruders would be waiting to pick her off.

Then, with a little shock, her numbed brain recalled why she and Thorn had come to the dock. To test the underwater breathing device. Had her dive dislodged them?

Lifting a shaky finger toward her face, she felt her nose. One plug had survived the dive. Still, the idea of drawing in water was terrifying.

Finally she had no choice. The filter was either going to work, or she would drown, because she'd never make it to the surface in time. Pressing the other side of her nose closed, she dragged in water through the remaining filter.

To her everlasting astonishment she got only air. Marveling, she exhaled and pulled in another breath. For a grateful moment, she let her body drift in the water. But she was afraid to linger. What if the intruders saw the telltale bubbles rising to the surface?

With a grimace, she struck out again, hoping she was heading along the shore and not out toward the middle of the river. She wasn't a marathon swimmer. In fact, she was already way past her fatigue level.

When she finally kicked upward and cautiously raised her eyes above the surface, the boat was about a hundred and fifty yards away, cruising in a slow circle. One of her attackers stood and pointed his gun toward the water, the other bobbed up beside the boat.

With a gasp, Cassie quickly submerged. When she chanced another look, she saw Thorn in custody, sitting between the other two men.

There was nothing Cassie could do but dive again and strike out for shore. Moments later, she heard the engine rev. Then she was alone in the cool water.

When the boat was out of sight, she headed for the beach. Reaching the Stones's estate, she stopped and set the sensors. Locking the barn door, she thought with an angry pang as she took the path to the house.

A minute later she was talking to Jason on the

phone, trying to stay calm enough to explain what had happened.

"We'll be down there in a helicopter as fast as we can," he told her.

"Don't come here. Try to stop the boat with Thorn."

"Okay," he promised. "But Cam and Jed are on their way to you. Meanwhile, get a gun and lock yourself in that room Trav uses for a gym."

"All right." Cassie ran her hand through her hair, mildly surprised that it was wet. With a little sob, she looked down at the bathing suit Thorn had admired. The feel of the damp fabric against her skin was suddenly intolerable. Grimacing, she found her T-shirt and shorts and changed quickly. Then she grabbed one of the pistols Jason had left with them.

But the simple tasks had sapped her energy. She felt drained, empty. Forty-five minutes later when Cam and Jed called her name and knocked on the gym door, they found her lying on her side on the quilt-covered exercise mat with her knees drawn up to her chest.

The looks on their faces confirmed the fears she'd been trying to hold at bay. Yet she still had to ask the question. "Thorn's gone?"

Jed shook his head. "We searched the immediate area. Jason's in another copter over the bay."

She still clutched doggedly to a shred of hope, until Jason arrived and confirmed that the boat with Thorn and the kidnappers had vanished.

"They must have been picked up by another craft. Or a seaplane," Jed muttered.

Cassie longed to pull the quilt over herself and close her eyes. She rubbed her face against the silky fabric that still smelled like the oil Thorn had been using to massage her. If she wrapped herself in the quilt, she could pretend he had stepped out of the room, and he'd be right back to hold her and tell her everything was fine. She ached to lose herself in that fantasy. Instead, she let Jed lead her to the living room where she huddled on the sofa and stared out at the water. Incredibly, the sun was still shining—sparkling invitingly on the waves.

"I knew we were in danger. I should have kept Thorn inside the house," she berated herself. "Or maybe we should have moved to another location after the first week."

"It's not your fault. We all thought he was safe. Tell me what happened."

It helped to talk. She didn't start to cry until Katie and Jo arrived by car. The sight of Jo's pregnant shape finally did her in. Weeping, she collapsed into her friend's arms.

"It's all right," Jo soothed. "We'll get him back."

"Oh, God, I'm so afraid." Cassie sobbed, unable to contain the anguish churning inside her. "For Thorn. And for the baby."

Katie and Jo stared at her. "What did you say?" they both asked.

She struggled to marshal a coherent answer. "I—I'm almost positive I'm pregnant."

Katie knelt beside her. "You missed your period?"

"Yes. And...and there are other signs. You know the way you feel bloated and your breasts hurt right before you get it? That hasn't gone away."

Katie nodded. "You should have told me, honey."

Cassie raised her reddened eyes. "I know. But what do you do when your most cherished hope and your worst nightmare are twisted together? I've been scared to think about it. Or talk about it. Because...the baby could have the same sickness as Thorn," she choked out. "And I could lose them both...." The end of the sentence dissolved in a storm of anguished sobs.

Jo rocked her. Her tears flowed freely. Finally she was too worn out to keep crying. Katie patted her shoulder and handed her a tissue. She blew her nose and wiped her eyes. Drawing up her knees, she sat with them pressed protectively against her body, a mother sheltering her child from harm.

"There's a good chance the baby will be fine," Katie said.

"How?"

"Half his genes come from you. And you've obviously got immunity."

Cassie hung on to that like a drowning swimmer clutching a life preserver.

"We'll do some blood work as soon as we get back to Baltimore."

"I...I guess there's no use staying here," Cassie whispered, looking around the rustic living room. Even with danger always hovering in the shadows, she and Thorn had spent their happiest time here. Made love. Argued politics and religion. Discussed everything from philosophy to Batman and voodoo economics. Lord, what if it was the only time they were going to have? She clamped her teeth together, unwilling to admit that possibility.

Jed moved from the doorway into the room. "You'll stay with us," he informed her.

"I—I don't know," Cassie said in a small voice.

Jed looked at her questioningly.

"You and Marci are so lucky to have each other. I know it sounds awful, but I don't know if I can stand to be with you," she admitted and swiped her hand across her eyes.

"I'm sorry," Jed muttered.

"It's not your fault."

He began pacing back and forth across the carpet. "Damn. We should have put some kind of transmitter on Thorn."

"Don't blame yourself," Cassie told him, glad that she could comfort someone else. "We all made mistakes. I—I should have told him about the baby. Now I may never—" She stopped short and lowered her eyes.

"We'll get him back," Jo murmured.

"How?" Cassie demanded.

Jed stepped forward. "First we'd better establish that Montague's got him."

THE ISLAND was beautifully landscaped with plants that must have been imported from around the world. The house was a gleaming white villa with a red tile roof. And the property was patrolled by armed guards.

Thorn gave a little sigh as he looked down at the crisp oxford shirt and pressed slacks his host had laid out for his arrival. Both were the perfect size. He'd changed without comment, knowing the expensive attire created a more polished image than the rumpled T-shirt and shorts he'd been wearing on his arrival.

He didn't have much practice playing roles. In fact, if he'd been better at hiding his feelings, he wouldn't have gotten in trouble with Lodar in the first place.

But he'd had centuries to contemplate his past errors. He knew that three things were imperative in the present situation. To appear that he had the upper hand. To find out what Montague wanted. And to conceal any hint that his physical condition was deteriorating. He'd hid it from Cassie, and surely he could do the same with Montague.

Secretly he'd had some talks with Jed Prentiss about what to expect if he was captured. After assuring him it wasn't going to happen, Jed had been forthcoming about what it was like to be the reluctant guest of a man with absolute power. Now Thorn was very glad he'd listened attentively. He hoped he looked relaxed as he sat in an easy chair in Montague's study, sampling a tasty assortment of delicacies brought by a uniformed butler. He wasn't going to tell his host why it was imperative that he eat enormous quantities of rich food.

Crossing his right leg over his left, he made a point of not looking for the video cameras that were doubtless observing him. For good measure, he washed down some caviar with several sips of mineral water.

He was sitting in a creamy white chair next to a colorless tile table. Even the rug was off white. Apparently Montague was very fond of the color. Even the flowers in the garden had been white.

Thorn looked up inquiringly as he heard the turn of a doorknob. A short man dressed in a silk shirt and slim trousers came forward. He was small and precise looking with neatly combed dark hair and a pencil-slim mustache. He appeared much younger than Thorn had expected. Perhaps in his early forties.

"At last," Montague said, his voice tinged with a mixture of awe and triumph. "A very great pleasure to meet you, *monsieur*. How do you like our world?"

"I find it violent."

"*Oui.* I'm sorry."

"Like your methods in getting me here," Thorn parried.

"I apologize for the show of force."

"Why did you not simply ask?"

The Frenchman gave him a small smile. "I was afraid you might not accept my humble invitation."

Thorn studied Montague's confident carriage, his arrogant face. Zeke had speculated that he wanted to use Thorn's supposed power to control the world. "You could have gotten me killed."

"Never."

"Who was shooting at our plane?"

Montague's face darkened. "Lenov, the imbecile."

"Well, you're spared the task of disciplining him."

"*Oui.*" Montague changed the subject. "You've surrounded yourself with a group of protectors. Including the woman travel agent. Miss Devereaux."

Thorn's stomach knotted. At all cost, he must keep Cassie out of this. Keep her safe. Taking a small sip of mineral water, he tried to find out exactly how much Montague knew. "As you might imagine, her friends have been very useful to me while I picked up as much information as I could."

"Ah."

"But they are naive when it comes to profiting from my unique experiences. Did you bring me here to discuss some sort of business proposition?"

"You're very direct."

"I have little time to waste," Thorn murmured. "How did you find me? Did one of the group betray my location?"

"Yes."

Thorn's mouth went dry. "Which one?"

"Zeke Chambers."

Thorn couldn't mask his disappointment. He had trusted the man.

"I had the project chief call him to find out why he dropped out of circulation. I listened in on the conversation. Chambers's answers were evasive. So I knew he was up to something. Then all I had to do was keep tabs on his contacts."

So Zeke hadn't been at fault. Thorn took a bit of comfort from that. Montague seated himself in the chair across the table. "There are so many things I've been longing to discuss with you."

"Hmm."

"You were asleep almost three thousand years. You may not be aware of all the important developments that have transpired in the meantime. But the pyramid at Giza with its uncanny forecast of world history and ultimate destruction was already built before your people arrived on earth."

Thorn gave a guarded nod.

"Interesting how many religious traditions and seers predict the end of the world, isn't it?" Montague went on with controlled excitement. "The Norse concept of Ragnarok, the Hopi Indian belief that when the gourd of ashes drops, the end of the world is near."

Thorn steepled his fingers. Since Zeke had told him Montague was interested in religion and mythology, he'd been reading voluminously in the field. Ragnarok was the great final battle. But it was followed by rebirth.

"Or take the great seers Nostradamus and the American Edgar Cayce," Montague continued. "Nostradamus predicted the appearance of Napoleon and Hitler on the world stage. They were to be followed by another with even greater destructive force."

He bit back a remark that Nostradamus's cryptic predictions were open to interpretation.

"And now you're here to fulfill the prophecies."

Thorn hoped his expression didn't reflect the horror that dawned on him. It sounded as if Montague thought he'd been awakened so he could destroy the world.

"I've been looking for you ever since I found the tablets on the island of Corsica ten years ago."

"You are talking about specific references to me?"

"Yes. Written in Olympian. No one else was equipped to make the translations. But I had linguists spending years on the project. It was all set down in the Temple of Lodar."

"The temple of *what?*"

"I've reestablished the ancient rites," Montague murmured. "Here on this island stronghold, I have gathered a small group of followers."

Thorn stared at him.

"Men and women devoted to the ancient ways—the ways of your people."

Not my people, Thorn wanted to scream. Only a few who craved power.

"Do you know the original mission of the sect?" Montague asked.

"No."

"They were charged with the duty of keeping alive the secret knowledge of your return—passing it on from one generation to the next. Unfortunately for Lodar, the temple was destroyed by a tidal wave. It seems the very earth and seas conspired to hide your presence. But not from me. My hard work and diligence has paid off.'' Montague opened a drawer in the table between them, removed a remote control and pushed a button. A section of the wall slid aside, and Thorn caught his breath as several lighted cases were revealed. One displayed the missing artifacts that Zeke had photographed. The other held equally ancient tablets. But they were cracked and broken, missing pieces.

Thorn crossed the room and read the mangled text. It was a frightening interpretation of his role in future history.

''He names you as the agent of man's destruction,'' Montague murmured. ''And seers down through the ages have confirmed your role.''

Thorn swallowed. Seers down through the ages? What nonsense! Yet Montague had fitted it all into his warped hypothesis.

Thorn stared at the warning Lodar had left. The only saving grace was that the tablets were shattered so badly that the notations about his location were obliterated. So Cassie had gotten to him first. Not Montague.

When he turned back, the Frenchman's eyes were bright. ''Lodar wanted to deny you power,'' he said. ''But you will wreak destruction on this wicked planet.''

Thorn gave the madman what he hoped was a complacent smile. ''Yes. You've done an excellent job of interpreting the ancient texts—and the historical prophecies.''

Montague shrugged modestly. ''If you will permit a question, I want to ask you about one of the artifacts

Lenov brought. Something that Zeke Chambers didn't find because it had slipped into a crack in the floor."

"Of course."

The Frenchman opened a wall safe and returned holding a glass vial. The stopper was missing, and the contents were dried onto the inside surface.

"Do you know what this is?" Montague asked.

Thorn struggled to retain his calm veneer, to hide his horror. "A very powerful poison," he answered with a swift lie.

The megalomaniac's eyes danced with excitement.

Thorn turned away, afraid the horror would show on his face. His blood had run cold when he'd recognized the healing symbol etched into the glass. It was the vaccine that would have saved his life. Only it was completely useless now.

CASSIE TWISTED HER HANDS in her lap as she sat in the lounge at Medizone, the laboratory Katie and her husband. Mac McQuade, owned.

They'd been here for hours, running medical tests. So far, the only thing she knew for sure was that her pregnancy was confirmed. Still, she felt like a parachutist in free-fall—and the ground was looming closer and closer.

"How much longer?" she asked, remembering that it had been several days before the tests on Thorn's blood had been completed.

"With Thorn, we had to determine which protein the antibody bonds to," Katie replied. "But since we already have that information, we'll have some answers about the baby pretty soon."

Cassie nodded tightly.

The minutes ticked by.

The phone rang and Jed confirmed that a man fitting Thorn's description had been transported from BWI to Montague's island.

Jo sat on another couch pretending to read a magazine. Jed started pacing back and forth.

Cassie pressed her knuckles against her lips. She couldn't take her feeling of helplessness waiting a second longer. She had to do something. But not here. She needed to be alone.

Abruptly she stood. All eyes turned to her. "Excuse me for a few minutes," she murmured.

There was a small enclosed courtyard in the center of the building. Not Thorn's courtyard, she thought with a little pang as she stepped into the twilight. But she could smell the scent of flowers, even if the tears in her eyes blurred their colors.

Sinking to a wooden bench, she bowed her head and clasped her hands. It had been a long time since she'd prayed. Years ago, she'd given up asking for divine intervention in her life. But this was different.

"Please, God. Can you hear me?" she asked through her tight throat. It felt strange to be doing this. Yet somehow right. "Thorn has come so far. He's been through so terribly much. He's lost his children. Everything he loves." She gulped and struggled to keep from breaking down. "Now I'm carrying his child—and he can have a second chance. Please, he's such a good man. That's what got him in trouble in the first place. But hasn't he survived for a purpose? Isn't he here to do something important for mankind?" she asked in a small voice. "If you bring him back, I'll make up for all the things he's lost. I'll be at his side, doing everything I can to help him fulfill his destiny."

Her throat felt as raw as when she'd been in the fire. She tightened her fingers until they ached. "So is it asking too much for you to save him and the baby? Even if my reasons are terribly selfish," she added in a whisper.

Her tears flowed then, but she kept speaking, because she had to be honest. You couldn't lie to God and expect him to grant your prayers. "I waited all my life to find Thorn. I love him so much. I need him. Please."

Finally there was nothing to do but sit in silence. A little while later, the door opened and Cassie felt her whole body tense.

Katie came swiftly toward her. "I've been looking all over for you."

"And?" she managed to ask.

"You're producing antibodies that will protect the baby," she announced.

"Thank you, God," Cassie breathed. It was as if one of her prayers had been answered on the spot.

But along with the flood of gratitude came a terrible guilt. "If my antibodies will keep Thorn's child from getting sick, could they cure Thorn, too?" she choked out.

"I hope so," Katie said in a quiet voice.

Cassie caught the immediate import of the words. "Then he should have already gotten them. I was so stupid!" She raged. "I should have let somebody know—instead of worrying in silence."

"We can still do it," Katie said.

"If we can rescue Thorn in time—" It was impossible to go on.

Katie patted her shoulder. "We'll make it. Meanwhile, the delay will give us time to strengthen the concentration.'' With a comforting arm around Cassie, she led her back to the lounge.

The moment she spotted Jed, she ran to him. ''Can you make a raid on the island? Scoop up Thorn the way Montague did?''

''Lord, I wish we could. But it would be a suicide mission—unless we can figure out some way to get a message to Thorn. If he could neutralize those land mines, it would make all the difference.''

Cassie grabbed his arm. ''There may be a way I can contact him.''

''How?''

She looked down at her hands. ''There's something else I haven't talked about, because I knew it would sound...strange.'' She swallowed. ''Thorn and I have been sharing our dreams.''

''Shared dreams?'' Katie asked, her face skeptical.

''Sleeping, we have experiences together—that we both remember afterward.''

''But it happens when you're in the same room, doesn't it?'' Jo asked.

''That's true now.'' Cassie took a little breath. ''But the reason I ended up in Alaska was that Thorn was communicating with me before we met. I had a kind of compulsion to find him, although I didn't understand it at the time.''

Jo nodded. The others didn't look quite so convinced.

''I could try reaching out to him,'' Cassie continued.

Katie still looked a bit uncertain.

''It's worth a try,'' Jo argued.

''Can you give me something to help me sleep?''

Cassie asked. ''Something that's safe during pregnancy.''

''Yes. But let's not jump into anything without thinking it through.''

Cassie's eyes were bright. ''I'm going to try it whether you help me or not. I want to know he's all right. And...and I want to tell him about the baby,'' she said fiercely.

Jo nodded her agreement. ''I know. But this is so important that we have to use it to our best advantage. If you can reach Thorn, we can find out vital information from him. Like the layout of Montague's fortress, for example. And the man's vulnerabilities. Then we can give him instructions that could make a crucial difference when we storm the place.''

Cassie hugged her arms around her shoulders. Oh, Lord. Saving Thorn's life might depend on her being able to dream with him again. What if she couldn't do it?

Chapter Fourteen

Despite the sleep medication, Cassie's heart was thumping like a drum.

"How do you feel?" Marissa whispered. She was sitting in a chair pulled close to the bed.

"Scared," she answered brokenly. "I love Thorn so much...."

"I know, honey." They shared a long, poignant look. "You've got so much to deal with," her sister murmured.

"I waited so long to find a man I could trust. You and I both did."

Marissa nodded tightly. "But before that, we both did whatever it took to survive. We're strong."

"I used to be," Cassie whispered. "But what if I never see Thorn again? What if I never get to tell him about the baby?" she ended with a little sob.

Marissa squeezed her hand. "We've put a lot of pressure on you. But really, we've got a good shot at rescuing him even if—"

Cassie cut her off with a hollow laugh. "Don't. I know I'm playing a crucial role in this." She moved restlessly on the bed. "But I'm not sure I can even fall asleep."

"You can do it," Marissa said with conviction. "Do you remember those self-hypnosis techniques Sabrina taught us a few years ago when we were both worried about getting the travel agency started?"

"You mean when business was the most important thing in our lives?" Cassie asked.

Her sister smiled sadly. "Yeah. But you can still use the hypnosis drill—to help yourself sleep. Reinforce the idea of communication with Thorn."

Cassie nodded. "Thanks."

Marissa hugged her. Then she exited the room and quietly closed the door. The moment her sister left, Cassie was alone again with her terrible fears.

THORN WAS BONE WEARY. Exhausted from the long trip, exhausted from the endless conversation with Montague. It took a lot of energy pretending to be an invincible alien god.

Still, he'd worn Montague out. The man was sleeping. He'd gone to bed thinking he and the space traveler were deeply committed to the same goals. So he'd given Thorn access to the computer.

Now he sat hunched over Montague's processor—raiding every restricted-access file he could find. But fatigue threatened to blind him, causing the screen to blur and the images to jumble. Maybe he could just close his eyes for a moment.... But sleep proved too enticing a seductress.

CASSIE LOOKED at the lighted dial of her watch. It was still an hour before midnight in Maryland, but it would be very early in the morning in Europe. Thorn should be sleeping soundly, she told herself.

As Sabrina Barkley had taught her several years

ago, Cassie tried to clear her mind of all the things that worried her. She couldn't totally banish her fears, but she went ahead with the process, anyway, raising her eyes to the line where the wall met the ceiling. It was the best place to focus when going into a self-hypnotic state.

"Relax now," she whispered to herself. "Relax now."

The phrase was the trigger Sabrina had suggested. Almost at once, she felt the familiar tingling sensation in her face and hands that signaled she was changing to an altered state of consciousness.

So far, so good. At least she hadn't lost the knack. Feeling more confident, she deepened the trance, pretending she was slowly walking down a flight of stairs to the ground floor of a house.

When she reached the lower level, she gave herself a directive. "You're going to fall into a wonderfully refreshing sleep," she told herself. "When you do, you will send your consciousness from this room. Across the ocean. To Thorn. To the man you love."

THORN SAT DOZING in front of the terminal, dreaming of Cassie—reaching out toward her. For a few joyful seconds it seemed as if she were standing beside his chair. She was here! He could hold her in his arms one last time. Then, with a start, he jerked awake.

Confused, he stared at the computer screen through a hazy blur. It was all he could do to read the little clock in the upper righthand corner. He'd been asleep for fifteen minutes.

His vision was still cloudy. Raising his hand, he rubbed his burning eyes. The symptom meant the illness was progressing.

He'd hoped he and Cassie might have a few more weeks together. But he was never going to see her again. The terrible realization sliced though him like a jagged blade mangling vital organs. He loved her so much. He took cold comfort knowing she was probably better off without him.

Letting go of her gave him a strange sense of freedom. There was no reason to fight for his own life. And that meant he was at liberty to use any means possible to stop Montague.

But he had to drag himself through the next few days—and keep the Frenchman from knowing anything was wrong with him. Leaning back in the chair he took several slow, deep breaths. He wished he had access to the healing supplies he'd brought from the facility in Alaska. Or even the pills Katie had given him.

Almost certainly there was a medical facility in this fortress. But he couldn't admit he needed anything. With a sigh, he reached for a slice of the cherry cheesecake he'd requested from the kitchen—as if he'd simply been indulging a whim rather than fighting to keep his strength up.

Actually, it wasn't so bad for a last meal.

CASSIE FOUND HERSELF standing in a long corridor with very white walls. She knew she was dreaming.

For a moment she'd caught a glimpse of a room. An office with a desk and a computer and Thorn sitting in a chair. Sleeping. Eagerly, she'd reached toward him. But he'd vanished, leaving her alone in this place she'd never seen before. Lord, she hoped she'd made it to Montague's fortress.

"Thorn?" she called in a quavery voice.

He didn't respond, and she felt goose bumps rise on her skin. This wasn't like stepping out into the sunlight and looking down on Thorn's garden, knowing he was waiting for her even though she couldn't see him.

She had no idea where to find the office with the desk and the computer. If that was where he really was.

"Thorn?" she called again, his name ending in a little choking sound. What if someone else stepped out of the shadows?

But no one replied. A chill breeze stirred the hair on the top of her head. Was she really close to Thorn—or was this a place of her own making?

Feeling lost and alone, she began to tiptoe down the hall.

THORN'S FORK CLATTERED onto the plate. Every cell of his body screamed for sleep. The urge to relinquish his hold on consciousness was almost irresistible—as if an outside force were pulling at him—tugging at his mind, compelling him to obey.

Doggedly, he commanded his weary brain back to the material on the computer screen. Yet as he scanned the text, his skin began to prickle.

A new symptom?

As if from far away, he heard a noise like a shout.

His body went very still as he listened intently.

Nothing moved. No one spoke. His imagination was working overtime, he told himself.

He fought to stay alert. But his lids were much too heavy. His eyes drifted closed. From one beat of his heart to the next, he was asleep. Dreaming.

Suddenly there was no doubt about what he'd heard. A strangled voice was calling his name.

"Thorn."

Cassie. That was Cassie. In the hall.

He knew it was impossible for her to be in this place. Yet fear for her burned through him with white-hot intensity. He was out of the chair and across the room in two quick strides.

He burst through the door and found her standing in the hall.

"Thorn. Thank God. I thought you might not be here—that I'd made this place up."

Cassie, here! He looked at her in wonder. And he saw the same dreamy expression on her face. Capturing her in his arms, he gathered her to him. They held each other tightly, swaying back and forth, until he claimed her lips in a kiss that rocked him to his soul.

"I love you," they both gasped as they drew back to breathe.

She was crying. His hands shook as he brushed away her tears. "Don't, *dubina.* It is all right. It is all right."

"I prayed I'd hold you like this again," she whispered.

"Yes."

Her hands moved over his body. He couldn't stop touching her everywhere he could reach. This was a gift. A last gift he would cherish until the end. He was nothing more than a man holding the woman he loved. A woman he had crossed centuries and light-years to find.

He whispered the words that had been locked in

his heart. "I never thought it was possible to love so deeply."

Joy leapt on her face. Joy that made his heart melt. Yet he must not surrender the miracle of being with her.

"It is dangerous for you to be here. Even in a dream."

She held his gaze with her. "I had to come. I had to be with you, my love. Jason and our friends need to know about this place, so they can rescue you."

"I cannot leave," he said in a quiet voice.

"Thorn, please."

"Cassie, I wish things had turned out differently. The man who chased our plane brought Montague the container with the vaccine. But the flask is broken. The contents are useless. I am going to die. But I am going to stop Montague first."

She gripped him convulsively. "You can't die! Not after you've been through so much."

He shook his head sadly. "Hear me out. I must make my last days count. Montague has spent his whole life reading tea leaves and brewing disaster for mankind." Thorn snorted. "He has been looking for all sorts of outrageous signs that the world is coming to an end. In case I did not appear to fulfill the supposed prophecies, he has been supplying third-world countries with materials to make nuclear missiles. They do not know he can launch them and destroy key cities around the globe. Radiation would take care of the rest of the people—except for the followers he has gathered on this island."

The horror of it made Cassie go cold all over. "The radiation will come here, too. It will kill everybody."

"He has used Olympian technology to build a...a

force field.'' Thorn's eyes turned flinty. ''But I have convinced him that I have a more elegant way to end the world. By bringing up a system to expand the molten core of the earth and create volcanic eruptions all over the globe. Except here, of course. That way, there would not be any radiation contamination.'' He laughed harshly.

''He has given me complete access to his computer system. One of the things I have really done is give myself a quick course in force-field physics. It is not my area of expertise, but I have got a good enough technical education to understand the basics. I am going to get him to demonstrate the system for me in case we need it to block out volcanic ash. Then I think I can shrink the area down in size—so that only Montague is trapped inside. When he is safely snared, your friends can come in and scoop him up.''

''What about you?'' Cassie asked.

''I do not know.''

''Don't make plans that put you in danger. We have a way to save you without the vaccine.''

He shook his head. ''I am sorry. Katie's methods have only been temporary.''

''Thorn.'' She compelled him to look at her. ''My body is making antibodies that will cure you. If I hadn't been afraid to confide in Katie, we could have already given you an injection.''

''Your body? I do not understand. How—''

In the next moment, she saw the expression on his face change from perplexity to wonder.

''You are with child.'' His voice shook.

She gave him a cocky little smile just before he swept her into his trembling embrace again.

"I suspected. But I was so frightened that the baby might have the illness that I couldn't deal with it."

"I understand," he said, gently stroking his knuckles against her cheek, her lips.

"But he is fine. Katie tested my blood and found the antibodies."

His hand swept down her body to press against her still-flat abdomen. "You know it will be a boy?"

"No. I was using a convenient pronoun."

"Twins run in my family," he said in a husky voice.

"I'd like that. Or a boy now and a girl later. Or the other way around. Or any combination you like." She nestled against him. All she wanted to do was curl up with him in some quiet room and forget about the danger. But they had urgent work to do. "Jason and Jed are moving into place with an invasion force. We have to know where to find Montague—and where you'll be. Also, they want you to disarm the mine field, if that's possible."

"Different sections are activated at different hours of the day. But I think I can neutralize them."

"Good. Does the computer also have a layout of the fortress?"

"Yes. But how will you remember so much information?"

"When I get back, Sabrina is going to put me into a deep hypnotic trance. I'll have total recall," she told him, hoping that it would work as well as her friend had claimed.

Thorn led her to the office. For the next hour, they worked steadily. First Thorn took her on a virtual-reality tour of Montague's fortress and showed her his working files. Then they explored the communications system and designated a frequency they could use for radio contact.

"Jason told me they'd be ready for an assault as soon as it gets dark this evening," Cassie said.

"I cannot be sure that *I will* be ready," Thorn countered.

"Can't we help you? At least create a diversion?"

"No. If Montague thinks he is under attack, he could fall back on his original plan and launch the missiles," Thorn warned. "I must neutralize him first. Then I will give you a signal."

Cassie didn't like it, but she saw no option.

Thorn covered her hand with his. "*Dubina,* never doubt that I want with all my heart to live a long, happy life with you and our child. But if I believe Montague is going to launch the missiles, I must stop him. Any way I can."

A chill went through her. There was no mistaking what he was saying. To save earth from destruction, he was prepared to sacrifice himself.

"If you're in trouble, let us know," she pleaded.

Before Thorn could answer, his image blurred and wavered like a film projected onto an undulating screen. At the same time, the feel of his hand against her flesh became insubstantial—as light as the touch of a specter. Fear hit her like a lightning bolt. "What's happening?" she gasped.

Chapter Fifteen

''Montague is here,'' Thorn said in a hoarse whisper.

Cassie looked around and saw nothing. ''How?''

''It is morning. He has come in and found me slumped in the chair. Sleeping. I must wake. Immediately.''

''Wait.''

For an instant, Thorn's hand pressed tightly over hers as if he could somehow keep the two of them together forever. Then he vanished, and she was propelled into a dark, frightening void. She tried to scream, but the sound didn't reach her lips.

Her eyes blinked open; her face contorted, and she reached for Thorn. He wasn't there, and she sank back against the pillows of Katie's guest bed.

Sabrina, who had been sitting across the room, came swiftly to her side. ''What's wrong?''

The sense of loss was so terrible she felt as if her heart would burst from the pain. It took several moments before she could control her voice enough to speak. ''Montague woke Thorn out of our dream. I didn't get to find out what happened next.''

''But you talked with Thorn. He was all right when

you left," Sabrina said. "Did you got the information we need?"

Cassie tried to hold back her tears, but they trickled down her face. She wiped them away with the backs of her hands. "He's going to sacrifice himself to save the world. We've got to get him out of there."

FIGHTING A SENSE of disorientation, Thorn straightened in the chair.

"You fell asleep while you were working," Montague said in an accusing tone. "I thought Olympians required only a few hours rest."

Thorn raised his head and gave the man a narrow look. "To untrained eyes, what you saw may have appeared to be ordinary sleep. Actually, it was a trancelike state to assist in assimilating information."

"Ah. Can you teach me this technique?"

"I am afraid not. It is a skill my people acquired over thousands of years. But it uses up great quantities of energy. Tell your kitchen staff I must have food at once," he added in a tone he hoped was suitably imperious.

"I was about to invite you to breakfast."

"Good." Thorn rose and stretched, using all his concentration to keep from swaying on his feet. He was a lot weaker than when Cassie had arrived. If he couldn't wrap this thing up quickly, he might not make it.

When he caught Montague giving him a critical inspection, he forced a genial smile. "While we eat, I will tell you about the progress I have made on the volcanic core program."

The man's doubts appeared to vanish. "Excellent."

Still, Thorn didn't like the expression he'd seen in

the Frenchman's eyes. Montague was a dangerous man. Anyone who planned to trick him had better be on his guard.

"THEY'RE TESTING the force field, all right," Jason announced.

Cassie felt a mixture of elation and alarm. Was Thorn closer to putting his plan into operation? Or was Montague getting ready to launch the nuclear missiles? "How do you know?" she asked.

Jason favored her with an evil grin, and she saw the rest of the men in the room struggle to keep their expressions neutral. "I had a low-flying aircraft arrange to have an accident," he said.

"A crash?" she gasped.

"No. An unfortunate mishap with its chemical toilet. The waste should have landed in the middle of Montague's garden. It was deflected by an invisible dome."

The room erupted in wicked laughter.

"I'm glad you can still be amused," she said.

Jed gave her an apologetic look. "We've got to have our little victories—or go nuts."

"I understand. I'm not criticizing," she answered.

They were at a farmhouse Jason was using as a base in the Sicilian countryside. The team had been waiting for thirty-six hours for Thorn's signal. For Cassie, every second was agony. Thorn's time was ticking away.

Her fingers gripped the edge of her rush-seated chair, and the coarse fibers dug into her skin. The pain helped anchor her to the room where she sat.

She wanted to sleep, wanted to go to Thorn again. But she hadn't been able to reach him since she'd awakened in Katie's bedroom. Either he wasn't sleeping, or—

She didn't let herself go farther down that path. With a conscious effort, she straightened her back and tried to pay attention to what Jason was saying. She wasn't going to let the men see her anguish. She had to convince them she had her act together or they'd never take her on their raid. And she had to be there. She *had* to.

"FORGIVE ME, *mon ami.* I must get some rest," Montague said in a low voice.

Thorn ignored the satisfaction that leapt in his breast. Since his captor had surprised him sleeping in the chair, he'd been subtly driving the man, while getting him to reveal the extent of his knowledge and the details of his defensive and offensive systems.

"I understand human limitations. Why don't you take a short nap?" he suggested sympathetically.

"I hate to waste such valuable time. Conversation with you is so stimulating."

Thorn smiled warmly. *Of course the conversation is stimulating,* he thought with an inward sneer. *I've been encouraging you to brag about your achievements nonstop.* "It is all right to lie down for a little while. I can use the time to check out the satellite broadcasts," he said

Montague stood and walked heavily toward a small room off the office. "I'll catch a little shut-eye on the couch. Wake me in forty-five minutes. No longer."

Thorn murmured his assent and turned toward the bank of television screens along one wall of the office. As soon as the other man closed the door, he relaxed the iron grip he'd been exercising over his body. Immediately, a terrible feeling of weakness descended over him like a damp, heavy blanket. His arms felt glued to the chair. Drawing in a full breath made his lungs ache.

With an effort of will, he reached for the computer keyboard. Yet his hand wavered as he began to call up the force-field program. A mistake would be fatal. Not only for him. For the world.

THE COMMUNICATIONS CONSOLE crackled to life. "Delta Leader calling Sigma Unit. Delta Leader calling Sigma Unit."

"It's Thorn," Cassie breathed.

Jason bent to the controls. "Sigma Unit here."

"The containment field is in place. How soon can you be on site?"

"Half an hour tops," Jason answered. "Have you neutralized the mine field?"

"I have deactivated the master controls. And I have locked the doors to the barracks with the mercenary force. The building is heavily reinforced. But the troops may be able to shoot their way out."

"We'll be on the alert."

Cassie snatched the microphone from Jason. "Where are you?"

"In Montague's control center. The assault team knows the location?"

"Yes."

"Do not come with them." His voice was sharp, urgent. "That is an order."

"You've been keeping me out of there. But you can't give me orders."

"We do not have time for an argument," Thorn grated.

"Correct." She broke the connection and turned to Jason. "Let's go."

"He's right. You stay here. Someone else can give him the vaccine."

"No. You all have other jobs to do on the island. Let's go before it's too late."

THORN WAS METHODICALLY dismantling the island's defense systems when he heard a loud crash from the next room. It was followed by a richly descriptive curse in French.

"What have you done?"

Thorn looked toward the closed door. "You have been contained by the force field," he answered and turned his attention back to the computer.

"You're testing me?" his captor asked.

Thorn made a quick decision as he continued to pound on the ridiculous keyboard. "Yes," he answered. He'd hoped the Frenchman would give him the opportunity to work uninterrupted. Now he needed to buy some time.

"Let me out of here," Montague commanded.

Thorn continued playing the part of the haughty alien. "You dare to question my decisions?"

"I thought we were working together, *mon ami.*"

From the strain in Montague's voice, Thorn knew he was struggling to sound calm. Thorn reached to turn on the camera in the next room. An image of the captive leapt on to a nearby monitor. He looked furious, his hand raised to pound on the door. But the force field kept him from touching the wood.

"I do not appreciate the way you are using my power. How do I know that you will share the fruits of my labor?'' Thorn challenged as he surveyed the coastline defenses.

Apparently he'd used terms the Frenchman could understand. ''I appreciate your concern. But I would never try to double-cross an Olympian.''

''Convince me,'' Thorn insisted as he gingerly defused the mines at the perimeter of the island. Cold sweat beaded his forehead, and he had to squint to see the screen. ''Not now,'' he whispered. ''Give me a little more time.''

Montague's voice came to him—earnest, urgent, conciliatory. He barely listened.

However, when he glanced up, he saw that the man was also working while he talked. He had opened a panel beside the couch and pulled out a small computer terminal. Quickly, Thorn tried to extend the force field. But it was too late. Montague pulled the movable desk in front of himself and activated the terminal.

A camera swung toward Thorn. Montague had him on visual now. At the same time, Thorn's screen went blank. *''Klat!''* he spat out as he reached to restore his control.

''I'll kill you,'' Montague snarled. ''Even if I have to blow this place up. I was beginning to suspect I never should have trusted you. Lodar was right. You are unworthy.''

Thorn didn't bother with a response. He was typing the sequence that would neutralize the missile control program.

Montague cursed richly in French and moved to rescind the command.

Thorn overrode him, realizing somewhere in the back of his mind that he and the Frenchman were playing a computer game like the ones Cam had shown him. Only this was for real.

JASON POINTED OUT the window of the helicopter to a section of the beach where explosive charges sent water and sand shooting into the air. "Something's gone wrong."

He aborted the landing and moved higher. Still, sand pelted the bottom of the copter.

"Delta Leader," he called into the radio. "Do you read me, Delta Leader?"

"Stay away from the coastline." Thorn's voice came over the earphones they were all wearing.

Jason's voice remained cool. "We already know about the beach. You have problems?"

"Montague has an auxiliary control console. I am trying to neutralize him."

Cassie's heart leapt into her throat. "Can you make the force field smaller? Squeeze him?" she gasped out.

"It is at minimum extension," Thorn answered. Then, "I have the copter on visual. Montague probably has the same picture."

"Should we back off?" Jason asked.

Thorn sounded resigned. "No. Now that he knows that he is under attack, you had better come in. Cut off the power at the main generator and satellite communications."

"Will do," Jed acknowledged.

"Montague may—" Thorn's communication was cut off.

"Delta Leader. Come in, Delta Leader," Jason tried again.

There was no answer.

Cassie looked down as the ground loomed toward the helicopter. They were almost over the garden. Had Montague gotten the mine field back on-line?

Jason must be wondering the same thing, because he hovered inches above the garden. But there was no real option. They had to go in.

Cassie's heart was in her throat as she watched Jed jump to the ground. The rest of his men followed.

Then they dashed across the garden. To Cassie's everlasting relief, no explosions went off.

But a burst of automatic weapon fire erupted from a structure at the edge of the compound. Jason spoke into the microphone. A second helicopter swooped in low over the building and dropped a bomb.

Cassie cringed away from the explosion. "Satellites are going to pick that up. You have a cover story ready?" she asked Jason in a strangled whisper.

"We've been sent by one international crime lord to neutralize another," he responded.

"Convenient."

Another copter swooped in, and a second assault team hit the ground, guns at the ready.

Cassie waited for her chance with her heart pounding against her ribs. There were still no explosive charges near the house. Thorn had come through for them!

While Jason was looking the other way, she slipped out the door of the helicopter and started for the control center at a running crouch.

"No," Jason shouted. "Come back. You'll get yourself killed."

She ignored him.

THORN BENT OVER the keyboard, his mind functioning on a cool, detached level. He was in a place partway between dream and reality, where nothing existed but the job he needed to do.

Montague had a better command of the system. But Thorn had one advantage. He was faster than any earth man. All he had to do was stay conscious long enough to see this through.

Glancing at the TV monitor, he saw Montague working feverishly. The other man glanced up at his own monitor—then returned to the keyboard.

Since Montague had activated the auxiliary controls, each man had managed to counter the other's moves. Barely. But Thorn was determined to come out the winner. He must!

The door from the hall burst open.

"*Klat!*" Thorn spun in the chair, expecting to find that one of Montague's guards had escaped from the barracks.

Incredibly, it was Cassie, dressed in combat fatigues. Not Cassie. Not here. He'd tried so hard to keep her out of danger.

"Go away," he grated.

"No." She hurtled across the room, just as the computer screen went blank again.

"Thorn, I have—"

"Later," he shouted, all his attention on the machine. "I must do this!"

His throat burning with fear, he kept trying keys. None of them worked—until he remembered the cancel command to an emergency shutoff sequence. He typed the complicated series of letters and numbers, and the screen sprang to life again. But his fingertips were tingling and he was having trouble feeling the keys.

"Please let me—"

"Cassie, I must...concentrate—" He saw that Montague was attempting to launch the missiles. With a grimace, Thorn countermanded the sequence.

When the immediate crisis was over, he sighed deeply.

Cassie looked at the television monitor. "He knows I'm here."

"That will not make any difference."

"Can you cut off his oxygen?" Cassie asked. "Inside the force field."

Thorn was thunderstruck. "Why did I not think of that?"

"You're not thinking like an evil alien."

He began to press keys, made a mistake and had to erase the line, cursing under his breath.

In the middle of the correction, he realized he could do better than simply deprive the Frenchman of oxygen.

"I can pump carbon monoxide from the exhaust system into the room," he muttered.

"Do it."

Thorn pushed himself as hard as he could, reversing the airflow in the other room and enlarging the force field to include the vent. Endless seconds passed.

The Frenchman made another attempt to get to the missiles. Thorn blocked the ploy, praying that the odorless gas would have an effect.

After what seemed like an eternity, the man's movements slowed. Then he slumped over the keyboard.

Thorn was about to thank Cassie when the screen and the monitors went dead. Blood froze in his veins.

Had Montague found a way to cut off this terminal—and initiate the destruct sequence—before he passed out?

Cassie's radio crackled. "We've shut off the power," Jed's voice came over the line.

"Thank you," Cassie breathed.

Thorn felt his heart rate slow a little. "Montague's in the next room," he told Jason. "You had better come and get him."

He wanted to say more, but the tremendous effort of the computer battle had taken its toll. He slumped back in his chair, looking at Cassie as if they were separated by layers of fog.

At least he had saved her and the people of this planet. He'd made up for the interference of the Olympians three thousand years ago. At least he had that satisfaction. He tried to pull himself erect, but he couldn't muster the energy.

"Oh God," Cassie cried out, fighting the panic that threatened to paralyze her. "Thorn, hang on. Please hang on. You can't die now. I won't let you!"

Her face contorted with anguish, she clutched the medical kit slung across her chest.

As she bent over Thorn, she felt the breath freeze in her chest. His skin was pasty—and covered with beads of perspiration. His breath was shallow and ragged. Then, his face contorted with a spasm of pain that wrenched at her heart. He'd fought so long and hard. It couldn't end like this!

"God, let him hold on," she prayed. "You can't give up on him now."

Thorn's eyes were closed. They opened slowly, and he squinted toward her as if he couldn't see properly.

Slowly, his hand reached for her, then fell back. "Cassie. *Dubina,* never forget that I love you."

"You'd better stay around to remind me!" Blinking back the tears that blurred her vision, she fumbled in a small case slung over her shoulder.

She was frightened, frantic. Yet some corner of her mind stayed very calm, like the eye of a hurricane.

"Take it slow and easy. Do it right," she intoned under her breath as she grabbed Thorn's arm, pushed up his sleeve and swabbed his skin with alcohol the way Katie had shown her. Then she pulled out a hypodermic, filled it from a small bottle and discharged a few drops from the tip.

"Hang on. Just hang on. This is what you need," she whispered as she plunged the needle into Thorn's arm. It didn't appear that he was listening. But she needed to keep talking, to stay connected every way she could. "It's going to take a little while for the antibodies to work. So you save your strength, do you understand?"

His lips twitched, and he made a small sound in his throat.

"I've also brought you some of the medicine Katie says will help. In liquid form so you'll absorb it faster." She uncorked a small bottle.

When Thorn didn't move, she lifted the vial to his lips the way she'd done when they'd first met at the station.

"Drink," she ordered.

Obediently, he swallowed, then grimaced. "Tastes awful," he muttered.

She considered the complaint a good sign. Her hand softly brushed back the damp hair from his forehead. Her lips moved against his cheek.

Then all at once, she was too weary to stand. Her legs buckled, and she grabbed the chair to keep from falling. Kneeling beside Thorn, she pressed her face against his knees and clung to him as best she could.

"You came all this way to find me. You'd better not leave me now," she ordered.

His hand moved to her shoulder, slowly inched toward her cheek, then went still.

She turned so she could move her lips against his fingers. It would be hours before she knew if she'd gotten here in time.

"I need you. And the baby needs you. He needs a father. And he needs to know his heritage."

She was willing to say anything, do anything, if it would only make a difference. "Please, don't let Lodar win. Show him you're stronger than he is."

Tears leaked from her eyes, but she couldn't stop. She had done everything in her power to save his life. Now all she could do was wait and pray.

OUTSIDE, THE BRIGHT Sicilian sunshine bathed the hills in blinding light. Inside the farmhouse bedroom, the shades were drawn.

Cassie rested beside Thorn in the old-fashioned rope-spring bed, listening to his breathing. It was peaceful now. An hour ago, it had been ragged. And when she'd tried to go to him in his dreams, she'd felt as if he'd erected a barrier against her. Because he was too sick?

That had made her chest tighten with fear and a deep, aching pain. She needed to talk to him. Love him. But the best she could do was lie beside him under the light covers.

Katie had said that if he made it through the first

twenty-four hours, he would be all right. It was almost to that deadline and she could hardly stand the tension.

He shifted, and she was instantly alert. Then his fingers touched her face. "Cassie."

She turned her head and gazed anxiously into his blue eyes. They were the clear, startling blue that she remembered so well. And they were guarded.

She felt light-headed. She wanted to pull him into her arms and hold tight—never let him go.

Instead she remained very still.

"How long was I asleep?" he asked.

"Almost a whole day. How do you feel?"

He stretched, his expression indrawn, considering. "Better than I have in a long time," he finally answered.

She let out the breath she'd been holding. "Thank you, God. Oh, thank you," she whispered. Then to Thorn. "You're going to be all right. You got the antibodies in time."

He looked relieved, but not entirely at ease.

"What's wrong?" she whispered.

"What happened to Montague?"

"He's dead. He tried to escape after we left and the attack force shot him."

"Good. He reminded me of Lodar. He was a man mad for power."

She looked at him with sudden insight. "Was *that* why you shut me out of your dreams last night?" she asked in a quiet voice. "Were you afraid he'd come after us again?"

"That is part of it. It is still a risk to be close to someone as unique as me."

She gave a little laugh. "I guess I can't accuse you

of an inflated notion of your importance. Not when you saved the world from destruction.''

His expression remained sober. ''What if someone else learns of the alien spaceman who was frozen in the arctic for three thousand years?''

''You weren't frozen. You weren't in the arctic.''

''That is how the story will be distorted. Or worse. What if another megalomaniac wants to use the spaceman's power? And if he will not cooperate, they threaten to do experiments on his wife and child?''

''His wife?'' Cassie breathed.

''You are not listening.''

''Yes, I am.'' She rolled to her stomach and moved over Thorn, holding him tightly, her face pressed against his shoulder, the backs of her feet covering his ankles.

She was gratified by his intake of breath and the way his body responded to hers. His hands slid up her legs under the light gown, across her back and buttocks.

''You're definitely feeling better,'' she murmured.

''My feelings have not changed. I love you. More than my life. But I have no right to ask you to risk everything for me.''

''I told you. We can build you an identity no one will question. We can live very quietly—anywhere you like. You can study our culture, our languages. Maybe you can write some bitingly insightful books about society, or you can come up with ways to solve our problems. And you can consult with Cam and Katie on bringing Olympian technology to market. No one has to know where it comes from. You can let people assume it was developed by Randolph Electronics and Medizone.'

As she spoke, she raised up enough to pull up her nightgown, rocking from side to side as she stripped it off.

Thorn said something partway between a curse and a prayer as she settled back against him, her naked body draped over his.

She moved her hips provocatively and raised her head so that her mouth could ravage him. "I'm not playing fair," she murmured between kisses that became steadily more passionate.

"No, you are not." He reversed their positions, his hands cupping and kneading her breasts, his mouth and fingers teasing and provoking as only he could do until she gasped out her need for him. Yet when he tried to end the sweet torture for both of them, she stopped him with her hands against his shoulders.

His eyes questioned hers.

She kept her gaze even as she gasped in steadying drafts of air. "Thorn, I've never felt this way with any other man. I've never felt safe enough to reach this level of physical need. I never knew that loving could be so powerful."

His expression became tender. "And I have never known how deeply I could care about a woman."

"Do you want to throw that away?"

"No. But I would never forgive myself if I brought harm to you—or our child."

She knew why he felt so strongly. He had suffered the loss of one family already and thought it was his fault. But she wouldn't let an ancient tragedy rule their lives.

"And I'd never forgive you if you disappeared because you thought I wasn't smart enough to make my own decisions."

"I was strong enough to fight Montague. I am not strong enough to fight you."

"I don't want to fight." The hands that gripped his shoulders pulled him to her.

He both surrendered and took command, kissing her, stroking her, driving her to jagged heights of passion that made her beg for mercy.

His eyes locked with hers—fierce and tender.

Then he was inside her, driving her higher until she was consumed by the shattering joy of fulfillment that radiated through her body and her soul.

Afterward, she snuggled against him.

"In your society, it is better for the child if the mother and father are married, is it not?"

"Is that another roundabout attempt at proposing?"

He laughed. "Do earth women always push the issue?"

"When they're desperate."

"Ah, well, I am working up my nerve to do this properly." He drew a breath. "Cassie, I love you. I traveled billions of miles and thousands of years to find one unique woman—you. Will you marry me?"

"Yes," she answered.

"I need you. Wanting to hold you again kept me alive. You are my anchor to this world. My guide."

"And the woman who loves you," she added, smiling down into the radiant blue of his eyes.

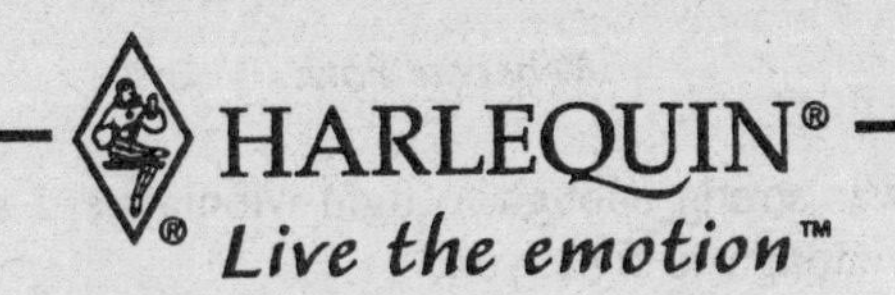

Heart, Home & Happiness

HARLEQUIN® Blaze™

Red-hot reads.

Harlequin® Historical

Historical Romantic Adventure!

HARLEQUIN ROMANCE®

From the Heart, For the Heart

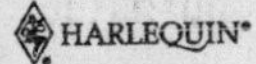

INTRIGUE®

Breathtaking Romantic Suspense

Medical Romance™...

love is just a heartbeat away

Next™

There's the life you planned.
And there's what comes next.

HARLEQUIN® Presents®

Seduction and Passion Guaranteed!

HARLEQUIN® SuperRomance®

Exciting, Emotional, Unexpected

www.eHarlequin.com

HDIR106

Harlequin® Historical
Historical Romantic Adventure!